I0522379

KING OF THE STREETS

a novel by

Maurice Hughes

Copyright © 2014 by Maurice Hughes
Published by Lethal Pen Publishing
P.O. Box 285
St. Louis, MO 63074
www.lethalpenpublishing.com
All rights reserved. This book or parts thereof, may not be reproduced in any form without permission from the author. This is a work of fiction. Names, characters, places, and incidents either are the product of the author's imagination or are used fictitiously. Any resemblance to actual persons, events, living or dead, or business establishments is entirely coincidental.

Printed in USA
First printing February 2015
Library of Congress Control Number: 2015902468
ISBN: 978-0-9861452-0-9

Acknowledgements

I would like to give thanks to our heavenly father. This book would not have been possible without you. To my family and friends; I truly appreciate all the advice, encouragement, and support you have given me during the development of this project. A special thanks to Niccole Simmons - 21st Street Urban Editing & Publishing.

I dedicate this novel to my cousin, Michael L. Terry II. May you rest in peace. You are truly missed.

CHAPTER 1

THE BEGINNING OF THE END

Two days after Kenneth's funeral, Trey sat in his bedroom peering out the window. Devastated by the death of his father, Trey closed himself off from the world. Not even his mother could reach him. Constantly visualizing memories of times they spent together, Trey could hear his father voice as he spoke to him. "Son, never hesitate. That could be the difference between life and death," he said while showing him how to aim a gun.

Trey's thoughts were suddenly interrupted by a knock at the door. His uncle's voice echoed as his mother opened the door. Leonard, Kenneth's oldest brother who always treated Trey like his own son, entered and hugged Elaine. A tear began to trickle down his cheek as Trey continued to think about his father. He watched a yellow and black butterfly softly float through the air near his mother's rose garden. He started thinking about how easy life would be if he were a butterfly. So carefree, no worries, no pain, but unfortunately, his life was not this way at all. Outside his room down the hall, Trey could hear the two of them talking about him.

"How is he?" Leonard asked as he sat next to Elaine on the love seat.

"The same. He stays in his room shutting everyone out. Trey won't even talk to the police."

Elaine began to shed a few tears, feeling helpless. Leonard watched her hold it together all throughout the funeral and knew it would eventually all come crashing down.

"I don't know what to do. I lost my husband, and now it seems as if I'm losing my son," Elaine said, crying as she leaned against Leonard for comfort. Leonard had no words, for he too was also having difficulties dealing with the realization that his brother was gone. After hearing his mother words, Trey realized that she needed him just as much as he needed her. In his mind, he could hear his father's voice again.

"Trey, she needs you. It's time to be the man of the house. I know you can do it. Don't let me down son."

"Don't worry dad, I will take care of everything," Trey replied as he stared at the picture of his father on the dresser.

Trey opened his bedroom door and walked down the hallway toward the living room. Standing in the corridor motionless, he could see his mother crying. "Mom, don't cry. Dad would want us to be strong."

Startled by Trey's voice, Elaine wipes away her tears.

"Baby, come here," she said with open arms.

* * * * *

Later that same night, Trey woke up and eased out of his room. He slowly crept down the hallway to check on his mother. He poked his head into her bedroom as he stood in the hallway. Elaine was sound asleep. Trey started down the staircase toward his father's study. Entering the study, Trey flipped on the light switch and approached his father's desk. He opened the bottom right desk drawer and stared at the velvet box for a second before removing it from the drawer. Trey opened the box and picked up his father's .40 Smith &Wesson pistol. The box also contained a suppressor. Aiming it at the wall, Trey visualized pointing the gun at Harold and New Jersey.

"Like my dad said, never hesitate. Harold you should have killed me because payback's a bitch."

*   *   *   *   *

Two Months Later....

Trey took a deep breath as he stood outside Harold's pool hall contemplating what he was about to do. His mind traveled back to the day his father was murdered.

It was a Saturday afternoon in May, 1994. Trey and his father Kenneth exited Shorty's Magic Market. Kenneth handed Trey a bottle of Stewart's strawberry soda after twisting off the bottle cap.

"You really love those, I see."

"Yes sir," Trey replied as he turned up the bottle.

Kenneth noticed Harold approaching him with his flunkies New Jersey and Silk. Harold stood about twenty feet away with a sinister grin on his face.

"Well, well, well, Kenny isn't this a quaint moment. You and your boy having a father and son day."

Kenneth sensed that Harold was up to no good. "Get behind me," Kenneth ordered Trey while slowly reaching for his gun.

Harold pulled out his nickel plated .380 and fired three shots at Kenneth. Pulling out his gun, Kenneth dropped to his knees after taking three bullets to the chest. His shirt was saturated with blood as he fell face first to the ground with gun in hand. Shocked at what he just witnessed, Trey dropped the soda and kneeled next to his father's body. Kenneth looked at Harold helplessly as he held Trey's hand, gasping for breath.

"Daddy, please don't die!" Trey cried as he watched his father die.

The three men laughed as Trey lays over his father's body crying.

"*Daddy, wake up.* It sounds as if you're a little punk ass bitch, just like your father," New Jersey said as he taunted Trey.

It was at that moment when time froze for Trey. He could hear the three men's voices, but his heartbeat was like a bass drum pounding in rage, a feeling unlike any he had ever felt before. Glancing down at his father's pistol, Trey looked up and noticed the barrel of New Jersey's gun pointed at his face.

"No! Don't shoot him. I believe the little dude got heart," Harold said as he admired the fact that Trey wasn't afraid of them. "Little man, what's your name?" Trey stood and stared directly at Harold.

"Trey," he answered with a bit of resentment in his voice.

New Jersey cocked his gun and pointed it at Trey. He didn't like the fact that some punk kid wasn't intimidated by him.

"Come on Harold, let me smoke the little bastard," Harold turned to New Jersey with a serious expression.

"I said let him be!"

New Jersey uncocked his gun and removed it from Trey's face. Silk and New Jersey were both surprised at Harold's decision to spare Trey's life. In his own twisted way, Harold could see a lot of himself in Trey.

"Trey, how old are you?" Harold asked.

"Fifteen."

"Look Trey, I know this doesn't mean much to you, but I'm sorry you had to see me kill your old man. I did what had to be done. Your dad had something I had to have and killing him was the only way to get it."

"What was that?" Trey asked.

Harold stooped over Kenneth's body and removes the gold engraved necklace from around his neck.

"Street Fame. Your father was the man on the streets, but now I'm the new king of the streets. Maybe after some time has passed, once you've gotten past this you can come work for me. I can show you how to make some serious cash."

"Yeah, maybe one day I will," Trey replied as he struggled to keep his feelings in check.

New Jersey stepped closer to Trey. "I wish you would have picked up that gun so I could have killed your little punk ass. Lucky for you, Harold let you live." Silk picked up the gun before spitting his chewing gum in Trey's face. "Now run on home and tell yo momma that your father is dead." Silk and New Jersey both laughed as they walked away.

*   *   *   *   *

Trey smiled as he thought about Silk getting killed in a shootout with the cops last week. "Pretty soon, your friends will be joining you," Trey said to himself while looking at the pistol tucked under his shirt.

Entering the pool hall, Trey kept his composure as he spotted several of Harold's men hanging around the pool tables shooting pool, smoking weed and drinking beer. New Jersey was standing outside of Harold's office as Trey made his way over.

"Little man, I see you decided to put the past behind you and come make some cash." Lighting up a blunt, New Jersey took a few puffs from it before offering Trey to take a hit.

Trey choked from the smoke New Jersey blew in his face. "I'm cool on that. I don't smoke."

New Jersey was offended by Trey's refusal to hit the blunt. "Well fuck you then, little nigga. I never liked your punk-ass father anyway. If it wasn't for Harold, I would have put a bullet in you and left you lying next to him. Just remember, don't fuck up! You don't want New Jersey to come gunning for your ass."

Trey refused to let anything New Jersey said rattle him. It was too late for fear. In his mind it was do or die.

"What, you ain't got nothing to say?" New Jersey asked as he continued to stare at Trey.

"Yeah, are you going to talk all day are let me through to see Harold?"

"You smug little punk," New Jersey said as he knocked on Harold's door before opening it. "Harold, guess who wants in on the game?" New Jersey said as he shoved Trey into Harold's office before slapping him on the back of the head.

Trey entered the office and observed Harold sitting behind his desk smoking a big cigar. He noticed the huge gold ring on Harold's pinkie finger. The stones on the ring formed the letter H. As he got closer, he noticed his father's gold chain around Harold's neck. Harold removed the cigar from his mouth.

"Have a seat. Can I get you anything?" He asked as Trey took a seat.

"No thank you," Trey answered as he glanced around the room.

Trey admired all the paintings on the wall - Frederick Douglas, Martin Luther King Jr., Malcolm X, Rosa Parks, Muhammad Ali and Scarface.

"New Jersey, give me a few minutes with the kid."

New Jersey pointed his finger at Trey as a gesture of shooting Trey. He walked out and closed the door. Harold placed his shiny black Stacey

Adams on the desk. He crossed his legs as he slumped down in his chair while continuing to puff on the cigar.

"So, I see you decided to take me up on my offer?"

"It depends on what you can offer me," Trey answered as he stared at his father's necklace. Harold sat upright in the chair. Putting the cigar down, he opened his top left desk drawer and pulled out a stack of banded, crisp hundred dollar bills.

"Trey, this is what separates boys from men," he said before tossing the money to Trey.

"What's the money for?" Trey asked as he ran his fingers across the bills while putting on his phony appreciation smile.

"I like to take care of my people, just my way of welcoming you aboard. That's if you are seriously considering joining us?"

Trey was intrigued to know what was Harold's angle. *Why would he extend himself to a kid that watched him gun down his father?* Regardless, there was nothing Harold could offer Trey that would make things right except his life. For Harold, it was all about business. He wanted to mentor Trey while introducing him to the street life.

Harold knew he lost a lot of respect on the streets from killing Kenneth in front of his kid. He was getting a lot of heat from the East and West side of Chicago. He knew he was marked but figured he could gain some leverage against Kenneth's crew if he persuaded Trey to join his organization. Trey laid the money on the edge of Harold's desk and walked over to the Malcolm X painting. Touching the painting, he slowly ran his fingers across the face of Malcolm X.

"I see you like that painting. It's yours if you want it. Son, I'm a busy man so I need to know what is your decision. Are you joining my family or not?"

Trey turned around and approached Harold with a sneaky smirk on his face. "Join you?" He laughed as he stood a few feet from Harold's desk. "Let me be honest with you. I didn't come here to join your family. I'm here to take back what you took from my father."

"Is that so? What, you want this chain?" Harold asked sarcastically flaunting the chain.

"Yeah, I want that too, but that's not what I meant. I came to get back my father's legacy. As you put it, his 'Street Fame'."

Harold laughed, not taking Trey serious. "Hold up, you telling me you came here to kill me?" Harold asked still laughing in amusement.

"That pretty much sums it up," Trey responded, staring at Harold with sheer hatred in his eyes.

"Okay let's say for a second I believe you. How do you intend on accomplishing this?"

"You really want to know?" Trey asked as he raised his shirt and pulled out the gun.

Seeing the gun pointed at himself, Harold finally had the smug grin wiped off his face. He could not have imagined the fifteen-year-old boy whose life he spared two months ago would come back this hard. Much less have the poise to walk into his pool hall make it past several of his men only to have him looking down the barrel of a gun. This was indeed a revelation for him. Harold could only hope that Trey didn't have the killer's instinct to follow through with his threat.

"Trey, you don't want to do this. Come on son, put down the gun and I'll forget this ever happened. I gave you two thousand dollars. You can have it. The money is yours to keep," Harold said as he tried to buy himself time to gain the upper hand.

"I know because where you're going you won't need it," Trey answered as he cocked the gun.

"That was your father's favorite gun. Do you even know how to use it?" Harold asked as he cautiously leaned forward toward the desk.

"I guess you'll find out soon enough," Trey replied as he was itching to pull the trigger.

Trey knew if he made the slightest hesitation, Harold would kill him for sure. "Did you check to see if the gun was loaded? Your dad never kept that gun loaded," Harold said as he pulled the handle of his top desk drawer and slowly opened it.

Pretending to be nervous and rattled, Trey noticed Harold easing his desk drawer open. Trey uncocked the gun and slid out the clip. Harold figured this was just the opening he needed. Harold opened the desk drawer and pulled out his gun. Trey put the clip back in the gun and cocked the gun.

"It's loaded now," Trey answered as he fired three shots at Harold, all making their mark in Harold's chest.

Harold dropped his gun on the floor as he leaned back in the chair feeling like his chest had exploded. He looked down at the blood pouring from his chest, and touched the bullet wounds. Harold could barely speak as he felt the life was being sucked out of him.

"So this is what it feels like to be shot. Little man how do you expect to get out of here alive?"

"The same way I came in here, walking," Trey answered as he approached Harold with gun in hand.

Standing over Harold with no remorse, Trey removed his father's necklace from around Harold's neck after watching him die. He shoved the chain in his front pants pocket.

"One down and one to go," he said to Harold before turning and heading toward the door.

Trey hid the gun behind his back as he opened the door. "New Jersey you better check on Harold. One minute he and I were talking, when suddenly he passed out," Trey said as New Jersey stared directly at him.

New Jersey noticed Harold slumped over face first on his desk. Concerned, he walked in as Trey closed the door. As he got closer to Harold, New Jersey tapped Harold on the back.

"Harold are you okay?" New Jersey forced Harold back into the chair. He saw the blood and bullet holes in Harold's chest.

"What the fuck! You little punk!" New Jersey said as he turned to face Trey. "You should have killed me when you had the chance," Trey said as he aimed his gun at New Jersey.

Trey was ready to blow him away. New Jersey reached for his gun but to no avail, Trey squeezed the trigger and shot New Jersey once in the right shoulder and again in right upper leg. Dropping his gun, New Jersey fell to his knees in pain.

"Look little man, we can work this out," New Jersey said, pleading for his life. Trey laughed after shooting New Jersey again in his left arm. "I would have never thought the big bad New Jersey would be on his knees begging and pleading for his life like a sorry ass bitch."

"It was Harold that killed your father. You killed him so we're even. Let's just put this behind us," New Jersey replied.

"Don't you think we're past that point? I watched you mock me while my father died in front of me."

New Jersey knew there was nothing he could say to get a pass from Trey. "Yeah that's right, and killing me won't bring your punk ass father back," he replied.

Trey stepped closer to New Jersey and kicked his gun away. He spit in New Jersey's face. "Stick a fork in yourself; you're done," Trey said before shooting him in the head, killing him instantly.

Holding the gun clutching it as if there were no tomorrow, Trey felt liberated. Tears began to trickle down his face as he talked to the gun as if it was his father. "Dad, I did it. Single handily, I avenged your death. Your legacy can live on. I'm the new king of the streets, and you best believe I will make you proud."

Glancing over at the edge of Harold's desk, Trey remembered the money Harold offered him. He stepped over New Jersey's body and picked up the money. Trey placed the gun back at his waist as he walked toward Harold's body. He figured there must be more money in Harold's desk. Trey spotted a briefcase underneath the desk near Harold's feet. He picked it up and opened it. To his surprise, he saw stacks of cash bundled up with three big bags of white powder on top. Trey smiled as he closed the briefcase and exited the office.

CHAPTER 2

THE NEW ERA

Fifteen Years Later...

It was 7:45am at the Coleman Towers. Six men dressed in all black, wearing ski masks armed with Uzi's and Tec-9's started up the stairwell. They entered the second floor accompanied by a police officer. The men approached apartment 2B. The police officer knocked on the door. Shasta, a pretty half African American and half Latino was on the phone talking to her cousin when she heard the knock at her door.

"Girl hold on. Who is it?" she asked as she approached the door.

"It's the police. I need to ask you a few questions regarding a series of recent break-ins that took place in the building."

Shasta looked through the peephole and saw the officer holding up his badge. "Shaquita, let me call you back. The cops are at my door."

Shasta unchained the door and opened it. She was stunned to see the six men wearing ski masks with guns pointed at her as they forced their way into her apartment. One man put his finger on her lips, gesturing for her not to scream.

"Please, don't kill me," Shasta begged as she fell to the floor and crawled backwards in fear.

Gunman 1 picked up Shasta's cell phone and glanced at the number of the last caller. He put the phone in his pocket as her three year old son, Chris, entered the living room.

"Mommy, what's going on?"

Gunman 1 stood over Shasta. He handed his gun to Gunman 2.

"Okay, this is how this will go down. If you want to live, you will do exactly as I say."

"What do you want from me?"

"I'm glad you asked. I want you to go to apartment 2G knock on the door and ask to use the phone."

"I know those guys in that apartment. They know I have a phone. What happens if they get suspicious?"

"Baby girl, that's your job to be convincing. Do whatever you have to do to get them to open the door. If you don't get them to open that door, I'm going to kill you and your son."

"I will do whatever you ask. Please don't hurt my son."

"Your son will stay here with one of my guys until we return."

Shasta was shoved out the apartment, and reluctantly started down the hallway as Gunman 1 and four other men trailed her.

*   *   *   *   *

Reggie and three of his men were sitting around waiting for the buyer to arrive to purchase the six kilos. Reggie's muscle, 1-Time, was sitting on the sofa with remote in hand, flipping the TV channels.

"Man, what's taking this dude so long?" 1-Time asked.

"Just chill, he'll be here," Reggie answered.

"Reggie, when I get my cut, I'ma jump down on this sweet ass pearl-white Escalade. Yo, I'ma bump it out with twenty twos and some halo lights." Chico, 1-Time's younger brother walked out of the bathroom.

"How many miles on that bitch?"

"It's a 2010 with about 22,000 miles on it. The dude asking 15 Gs for it!" Reggie laughed.

"Nigga you lying."

"No real shit!"

"Bro, if he's selling that Escalade for 15 Gs, then that bitch is either stolen or got a lot of heat on it," Chico replied.

"Or raggedy as all get out," Reggie added before laughing.

"Man, y'all niggas need to stop hating," 1-Time replied.

Suddenly, they heard a knock at the door. Chico walked toward the door and glanced through the peep hole. "Man, it's Shasta."

"Shorty got really bad timing. Get rid of her," Reggie replied.

Chico unchained the door and opened it. The gunmen burst through the door and began exchanging gunfire with Reggie and his crew. Gunman 1 stood over Reggie as he lay on the floor still alive but severely wounded. He removed the ski mask. Reggie could not believe eyes. "Man why would you do this? Why did you kill all my men? What is this shit all about?" Reggie asked.

Gunman 1 stared at Reggie for a few seconds before responding. "Nothing personal, just business. You can understand that right?"

"You will not get away with this. When Trey finds out, he'll kill you."

"Well, I don't have to worry about him finding out because you're the only one that saw my face. You won't be alive to tell him," Gunman 1 replied before shooting Reggie in the chest twice.

"Hurry up and get this shit and lets' go!" Gunman 1 ordered.

*   *   *   *   *

Shasta was waiting for the gunmen to return. She managed to crawl down the hallway once the shooting began. Gunman 1 and the others entered her apartment, and Shasta was horrified. She began to cry in fear thinking that after what she witnessed, they would surely kill her and Chris.

"Calm down sweetheart. I'm going to keep my word. You did your part so I'm not going to harm you or your son. Just remember if the police question you, your answer better be you didn't see or hear anything."

"I promise, I won't say nothing," she replied.

"Good, because if I or one of my associates have to come back we will kill you, your son and that bitch you were on the phone with earlier. Comprende'?" Gunman 1 asked.

Shasta shook her head in acknowledgement. Gunman 1 tossed Shasta her phone as he turned to leave.

"See you later, little man," Gunman 2 said to Chris as he rubbed his head.

The men exited the apartment. Shasta raced to the door and quickly locked it. She walked over to Chris and embraced him.

"Baby, I'm so sorry."

*   *   *   *   *

Meechi, Trey's right-hand man, picked up his cell phone and called Trey's hotel suite while driving down E. Chicago Avenue passing the Water Tower. Trey was in bed with two beautiful cocktail waitresses from his club. Shatina, Trey's favorite girl, was on top of him kissing his back while he was on top of Melody, a beautiful feisty Latino with long silky hair that hung down her back. She waited patiently for her turn as Trey pushed himself in and out of Melody. Melody, Shatina's friend and partner in this threesome, moaned in pleasure as Trey continued to go deeper and deeper inside of her.

The telephone began ringing. Shatina picks up the phone.

"Hello?"

"Shatina, what's up baby? It's Meechi. Let me speak with Trey."

"Meechi, Trey is busy. He'll call you back later," she responded in a nasty tone.

"Look trick, this is serious. Don't fuck with me! Put him on the phone," Meechi yelled after getting offended.

Reluctantly, Shatina rolled over after putting the phone down on the night stand. "It's Meechi. He insist on talking to you."

Trey's father's gold necklace rested against his chiseled chest. He rolled off Melody and sat up in the bed. He was a bit agitated after being interrupted.

"This better be important," Trey said after picking up the telephone.

"Trey, we got a big problem. You know the drop in the projects scheduled for this morning?"

"What about it?"

"Our guys were ambushed. All our men are dead and the word on the street is Donta orchestrated the hit."

Trey gave the ladies a hand gesture, signaling them to leave. Melody climbed out the bed. Her petite, perfect hourglass figure would make a cheetah faint. Shatina followed Melody as the two nude women headed to the bathroom.

"I thought we put that fool in his place. I see I've got to pay Donta a visit. Call him and set up a meet. Get Tony and the others and meet me at my club in an hour," Trey said as he motioned to hang up the phone.

"Trey one more thing, Monica called me this morning looking for you."

Trey ignored Meechi's comments and hung up the phone. Putting on his robe, Trey started toward the second bathroom just beyond the bar to take a shower.

"Ladies, I have some business to attend to, so I will see y'all at the club later."

Trey Wilkens, the self-proclaimed King of the Streets, lived up to his street reputation. He took his father's legacy and surpassed it by branching out to the entire Midwest. Trey became ten times bigger than his father Kenneth. Even the East and West coast drug lords were taking notice of how big Trey was becoming. But, much like everyone else, they were reluctant to start a war with the Midwest Kingpin.

*   *   *   *   *

After straightening out his tie, Trey stepped back from the mirror to check himself out in his Armani suit. He picked up the phone and called down to the front desk.

"Front desk," the hotel manager answered.

"This is Mr. Wilkens in the Presidential suite. Can you have valet bring my car to the front entrance?"

The hotel manager, Donald Stewart, was a medium height, bookworm male in his mid-forties. Donald was a bonafide ass-kisser at the likes of money.

"Certainly Mr. Wilkens, I'll have your car pulled to the front entrance immediately. Is there anything else I can do to accommodate you during your stay?" He asked while waving for Charles the concierge to approach the desk.

"If I think of anything I'll let you know," Trey answered.

Hanging up the phone, Donald checked the balance owed on Trey's suite.

"Charles, have the valet driver bring Mr. Wilkens' in suite 525 car to the front entrance right away."

* * * * *

Trey stepped off the elevator and headed toward the lobby. Donald spotted him and immediately rushed over. Donald grabbed Trey's hand awkwardly to shake it. "Mr. Wilkens, the valet driver should be pulling up with your car any minute sir."

Pulling out a wad of money, Trey put a hundred dollar bill in Donald hand before shoving him out the way.

"This is for your troubles, now get off my nuts!"

Trey entered the revolving doors exiting the hotel. Eric the valet driver pulled up in Trey's car. He climbed out of the two door, 2014 Pearl Blue Aston Martin with twenty inch, five star chrome rims and low profile tires. Eric gawked at Trey admiring his suit.

"Man, that's a dope suit. Is that Armani?"

Trey climbed inside his car as Eric held the door open. "That's right. Every player should own an Armani."

As Eric closed the car door, he thought about the cheap suits he had hanging in his closet. "Not me. I'd be lucky if I could afford their spend-off brand with the salary I make here," Eric responded, wishing he could trade lives with Trey for at least a day.

"You seem like a decent brother so check it. Whenever you're ready for a career change, come see me at my club. I can always use extra security," Trey said as he gave Eric a fifty dollar tip with a business card before driving off.

Eric glanced at the tip. "Damn, fifty dollars," he said to himself getting overly-excited as he watched the Aston Martin drive away. "Man, his license plates say it all." *HUSTLIN. Damn, I got to get my shit together,* Eric thought to himself as he looked at the business card.

*   *   *   *   *

Sergeant Turner enters the apartment. "It looks like a war zone in here," Sgt. Turner commented as he glanced around the room looking at all the bullet holes.

"This appears to be a drug deal gone bad," responded Officer Jackson. "Did any of the neighbors see or hear anything?"

"Everyone claims not to have seen anything," Officer Billups answered.

"I'm sure they had to hear all the shooting," Sgt. Turner added.

"All the bullets that went through these walls, it's surprising no one outside of this apartment was shot," Officer Jackson replied.

"These three jokers have rap sheets a mile long. Not to mention they're known associates of Mr. Chicago himself," Officer Billups added.

"Too bad he ain't lying next to these clowns," Sgt. Turner responded as he retrieved a pair of latex gloves from one of the crime scene investigators. He spotted a bullet casing just underneath the sofa. "Someone left their calling card," he said. "I want to know where this casing was manufactured, who sold it, who bought it and what gun fired it."

*   *   *   *   *

Monica looked at the clock as she rocked Trey Junior back to sleep. *Trey, where the hell are you,* she thought to herself.

One would ask why a sexy, classy woman like Monica would allow herself to get involved with the likes of a ruthless drug lord such as Trey. Monica was a gorgeous 29-year old interior decorator, and one of the finest young ladies on the streets of Chicago. Monica's luscious caramel brown complexion was enough to drive any man wild. Her perfectly structured body had all the men envious of Trey. Knowing she belonged to Trey kept the men at bay. They could only admire her from a distance. Any man that valued his life wouldn't dare step to Monica. Walking over to Junior's bassinet, Monica carefully laid him inside before hearing Trey's keys jingle as he unlocked the front door. As Trey entered the condo, Monica was standing in the corridor with a pissed-off expression.

"Well, I see you finally found your way home."

Seemingly unfazed by her comment, Trey laid his briefcase down next to the coat rack before taking off his jacket. "Sounds like you missed me," he answered.

His sarcastic remark only fueled her frustration. "Trey, where the hell have you been? I've been calling all over town looking for you."

Trey walked past Monica, entered the bedroom and approached the bassinet. "I was taking care of business," he answered after bending down and kissing his son on the forehead. "What did you want?"

"Well, let's see for starters, you're married and you should have brought your ass home last night!" She answered as she was getting even more agitated from Trey's nonchalant attitude.

Trey walked out the bedroom and headed toward the kitchen to get himself a glass of ice water. Monica followed closely behind him. "Yeah whatever," he replied as he picked up a glass and held it under the refrigerator's filtration system. Trey continued to tune Monica out but she would not let up. "Secondly, you act as if nothing's wrong."

After swallowing down the first glass of water, Trey refilled the glass. "See, this is the bullshit I'm talking about. Every time I walk through the door, all you do is bitch, bitch and bitch!"

Monica wasted no time striking back. "If you put in half the time with me and your son as you do with Meechi and your flunkies, we wouldn't have this issue."

"The only issue we have is you complain too much," Trey answered as he headed to the bedroom.

"Trey, I'm sick and tired of being here alone night after night wondering whether or not my husband is coming home," Monica added as she followed him.

Trey placed the glass down on the dresser and proceeded to the walk-in closet. "Well stop wondering. I was at the club most of the night," he replied as he picked out a suit.

"Trey, I'm not stupid. I know you were probably with one of those sluts from the club. You could have at least called, but I'm sure you were really busy!"

Laughing as he glanced at her through the mirror, he said, "See, that's why we don't fuckin' get along. You're so damn insecure."

"Okay, fine, since you think this is a joke, how would you like it if I start staying out all night?" Trey turned to face Monica after hearing her response.

"You know better so don't go there," he answered.

"I think I should. You are never here for us, and it's getting really old. Every night you don't come home, I ask myself, is he in jail? Is he with some whore, or is this the night I get that call from one of your goons telling me that you're dead."

"Me dead, now I know you've officially lost it," Trey replied.

"You know that you make enemies by the dozens. Mark my words, one day you won't think it's so funny," Monica added.

"Kill me? Please! Nobody has the balls to even try to kill me. These are my streets. I run the entire Midwest from Chicago to St. Louis all the way to Kansas. Don't shit go down without Trey Wilkens knowing about it."

Monica laughed knowing Trey was delusional for thinking no one had not even entertained the thought of attempting to kill him. "Trey, it can happen. Believe it or not, you are not God."

"Yeah, but I'm damn close," Trey answered.

"You are fooling yourself if you truly believe that. This arrogant attitude of yours will come back to bite you."

"What do you want from me?"

"Acknowledgement," Monica answered.

"What the fuck are you talking about?"

"You don't treat me like your wife, and you certainly don't give me the respect I deserve."

"Monica, I don't have time to listen to this shit," Trey said standing in front of the mirror dressing.

"For once in this miserable two year marriage, you're going to listen to me. When I agreed to marry you, you promised to love, honor and respect me. I guess after you got what you wanted all those promises went right out the window."

"Are you done?" Trey asked as he put on his pants.

"No! I know you think I'm not supposed to speak my mind."

"And yet you keep running your mouth," Trey added as he put on his shoes.

"Well believe it or not, I have feelings. Now let me educate you about feelings. If a woman is not getting the attention she feels she deserve from her man, sooner or later she starts to notice all the other men watching her."

Monica's words struck a nerve with Trey as he turns to face her. "What are you saying?"

"Just that I've had plenty of men compliment me. A few have even given me something to consider."

"Is this your way of telling me you've been creeping?"

"This isn't about another man. This is about you and me. Trey, I want you to know that I'm not going to keep taking your shit. Night after night, your son and I are home all alone while you're off at some hotel screwing some whore. Well listen to me good Mr. King of the Streets, if you can't show me the love that I deserve and change your ways, I will file for a divorce."

"Show you love? Don't I give you everything you ask for? Money, clothes, this fuckin' condo. Who bought you that damn Mercedes out front? All this jewelry, I bought all this shit! What about your hair, nails and toes getting done every week? Who's paying for that? Me, that's the fuck who! You never want for nothing. Your job ain't shit but a hobby. I pay for everything around here, so don't ever say I'm not showing you love," he yelled.

Monica usually held her tongue, but after putting up with Trey's constant disrespect, she decided no more. "You just don't get it do you?

Trey, I'm not talking about material things. I need your love. Marriage is more than just buying gifts and spending money. I need a full-time husband and Trey needs a fulltime father."

Feeling a bit of guilt as he tied his tie, Trey stood in silence as Monica words sunk in. "Look Monica, I'm here sometimes. You knew what my life was like before you married me. You talk about brothers pushing up on you. They better be careful. If I ever see you with any man while you're married to me, his family better start planning a funeral." Trey picked up the blue jacket and slipped it on before walking away from her. He headed out of the bedroom, through the corridor and into the den. Monica followed, still attempting to get her point across.

"See, this is what I'm talking about. You're always quick to want to kill somebody. Like I said before, you need to change your ways before it catches up to you. Is this what you want for your son? You want him to grow up selling drugs and killing people for a living, like his father?"

Trey had heard enough. He slapped Monica and she reeled backwards. "Shut the fuck up. If you can't deal with me being who I am then get your shit and get the fuck out! Now get off my mutha fuckin' case."

Monica could not believe that Trey put his hands on her that way. Monica was hurt, surprised and mostly in disbelief. She knew that Trey had a short temper but never imagined that he would ever hit her. Approaching the Malcolm X painting on the wall, just to the left of his desk, Trey pulled the portrait back revealing the safe. Trey kept at least fifty thousand dollars in cash on hand and several guns in the safe. The one thing that made Trey so successful in the drug game was his number one rule. Never bring work home. In tears, Monica watched as Trey retrieved one of his pistols from the safe. He picked up his favorite gun, the XDM 9mm and loaded it with one of the magazine clips inside the safe. Trey put the gun on safety before placing the gun down his front belt line. Closing the safe, Trey headed into the living room and grabbed his keys out of his jacket hanging on the coat rack.

"Where are you going?" Monica asked still tearing as she trailed him.

Trey turned and looked at Monica. He noticed tears coming down her beautiful cheeks.

"I have some business to take care of." Trey opened the front door and exited the condo.

"Mister Business Man, when are you going to handle your business at home?" Ignoring Monica's comment, Trey slammed the door startling Trey Jr. who began to cry. Monica tried to pull herself together. She wiped away the tears. Monica went into Junior's room and lifted him out of the bassinet. "There, there baby, Momma's here."

Trey reentered the condo. "By the way, don't forget the reunion is this afternoon. Wear something nice," he yelled before slamming the door again.

CHAPTER 3

WORD IS BORN

Trey pulled into the parking lot of his club. He saw his entourage standing around their cars waiting for his arrival. Meechi, a dark skinned powerhouse in his early thirties, was lying against the driver side front fender smoking a blunt. His deep voice and eagerness to kill keeps the entourage in line. Trey parked his car and approached Meechi.

"Did you do what I asked?" Meechi removed the blunt from his mouth.

"Yeah, I talked to Donta. He wants to meet at the Sand Pile."

Trey smiled in amusement.

"That figures. Somewhere he feels safe. Are you guys ready?"

"Let's do this," the entourage replied as they climb into their cars.

Trey walked up to Johnny's truck, a midnight blue Chevy Tahoe sitting on 22's. As he approached the driver side, Steve whispered to the other guys sitting in the back sipping on a half pint of Hen.

"Put that shit away."

"Johnny and Steve, I want you guys to stay a half mile behind the rest of us. Find a spot on each side of the perimeter and set up with scopes. Donta may be outnumbered, but he's not stupid. I'm willing to bet he'll have a trap waiting on us," Trey said as he turned to walk back to Meechi's blue Cadillac Escalade on 22's.

As Trey climbed inside, Meechi hit the power button and the speakers started to bump. He fired up another blunt, took a hit and passed it to Trey as they drove off.

*   *   *   *   *

Donta and his entourage prepared for Trey's arrival. The Sand Pile was a dumping site were all asphalt and construction companies came to load and unload salt, sand, rocks, and asphalt. Donta picked this place because this was his territory. He knew this was the one place that he could feel safe. Fearing that this sudden visit was more than just a social call, Donta sent two of his men to set up with semi-automatic guns. He figured if shit was going to pop off, he wanted to be ready. Tim spotted Trey's entourage approaching.

"Donta, it looks like we got company." Donta stared momentarily as Meechi's Cadillac approached with four other vehicles.

"Okay, I don't know what this is all about but if anybody reaches for their gun, everybody aim for Trey and Meechi."

Tim, Donta's right hand man, loaded his clip before placing it at his waist side. Tim had only been with Donta's entourage for six months. He replaced Terrace, who was killed by Trey eight months ago. Tim hated Trey. Everything he heard about Trey from Donta and on the streets made him want to kill Trey. Tim wondered how one man could be feared by so many. Deep down inside, he wanted to be Trey. He figured to be the man, he'd have to first defeat the man. Tim was not afraid of anyone and did not fear death. His 6'1", 290lb frame spoke volumes. Before joining Donta's entourage, Tim was a bouncer at Sexy Ass Strip Club.

"Don't worry, Donta. If Trey or Meechi even look like they want to reach, I'll smoke them both like a fat ass twenty sack."

"Alright, D-day is here," Donta said, taking a deep breath. "Everybody know what to do. Tim, make sure the shooters are in position," Donta ordered. Tim pulled out his cell phone to call Sam.

"Are you in position?"

Sam was standing on the roof top of the old Omni Steel Company with his HK MP5 in hand. The building had been closed for several years. Omni Steel was approximately nine hundred feet to the left of the Sand Pile. The view from the roof top overlooked the entire area. He was lying on his stomach in position when he heard his cell ring. He saw Tim's name on the phone. He laid down his gun as he reached for his phone.

"I'm ready," he replied.

Steve could hear Sam talking on the phone as he crept up behind him. He noticed Sam's gun lying beside him. Once Sam checked in, Steve slid a switchblade knife up to Sam's throat and cut him from ear to ear. Bleeding from the throat, Sam grabbed his gun rolled over to get a shot at Steve. Before he could get a good grip on the gun, Steve kicked the gun away and plunged the knife into Sam's chest, killing him.

"Nothing personal, homie," he said to Sam as he removed the knife and stood over him admiring his work.

*   *   *   *   *

Tim called Willie. "Willie, Trey and his entourage are approaching. Are you in position?"

Willie a short and stocky light skinned male in his mid-twenties was lying on his stomach on the rooftop of Crater's Plumbing Company. The building was a little over seven hundred feet to the right of the Sand Pile. He could see the entire layout of the Sand Pile except the rooftop of Omni Steel. Willie was holding his Uzi with a Wilson suppressor on it in hand looking down at Meechi's Escalade when he heard the call come through. He put down the gun and grabbed his phone.

"What up, Tim? I got that Escalade in my sights. Just say the word, and Trey will be a memory."

"Good. Stand by, wait for my signal," Tim answered.

Willie pushed *End* on the phone and glanced down at his new tattoo. Johnny was holding a steel chain as he crept up behind him and looped the chain around Willie's neck. Willie pulled on it as Johnny attempted to strangle the life out of Willie. Caught by surprise, Willie dropped his phone. Willie tried to pry the chain from around his neck. His face began to turn flush as Johnny continued to apply pressure with the chain. While gasping for air, Willie tried to reach for his gun. Johnny spotted Willie's arm stretching out as he attempted to grab the Uzi. He pulled Willie backwards, applying additional pressure. Willie attempted to mount one last surge of energy. He tried to stand but Johnny looped another portion of the chain around Willie's neck, tightening the chain more while dropping Willie back to his knees. Unable to free himself, Willie died in the struggle, falling face first on the rooftop. Johnny unwrapped the chain from around his knuckles and dropped the chain on Willie.

*   *   *   *   *

Trey and Meechi were sitting in the Escalade smoking the remainder of the blunt as they waited for Johnny and Steve to report in. Red and Tony were sitting in the back seat talking amongst themselves. Meechi's cell phone began to ring.

"Talk to me," Meechi said as he answered the phone.

"It's done. Steve and I have taken position."

Meechi glanced at Trey, giving him a head nod before responding. "Johnny, you and Steve keep your eyes on me. When I give you the signal, take out Tim," Meechi instructed before hanging up. Meechi took one last puff before passing the roach to Tony. "It's time to twist some caps."

Trey opened the door and stepped out of the car. His entourage followed his lead as they exited their vehicles.

"This muthafucka gon' regret stealing from me," Trey said to Meechi as he approached Donta and his entourage.

"Good old Donta. What ya know?" Meechi said as he stood a few feet away.

Donta was scared, and it showed as he knew Trey had bad intentions in mind. "I'm sure you guys didn't come here to socialize, so let's get down to business. What is this all about?"

Smiling, Meechi glanced at Tim who was staring at him as if he wanted to rip his head off. "Lighten up, this is just a social call. Tim, long time no see. You know, I heard you've been busy on the streets robbing junkies and hookers trying to make a name for yourself. With a fucked-up resume like that, you should feel proud to be standing with the big boys."

Tim knew Meechi was trying to get to him, but unfortunately his short fused temper got the best of him. He slowly started for his gun. Donta touched his hand gesturing not to do it.

"Don't let him provoke you," Donta warned.

Meechi opened the jacket to his Armani suit, flashing his gun sitting just above his waist line. "If I was you, I'd thank Donta for saving your life."

Donta felt they were not getting anywhere, so he turned to Trey.

"Trey, what is all this about?"

Tim momentarily forgot about his near shoot out with Meechi and locked eyes with Trey.

"Funny you should ask. This morning I was hit for six kilos down in the projects. You know I have eyes and ears everywhere. Rumor has it that you ordered the hit," Trey answered as he reached into his jacket pocket and pulled out a pack of cherry flavored Black & Milds.

"Trey, is this some kind of frame-up? I didn't have nothing to do with your missing kilos," Donta answered.

Trey lit his cigar and took two puffs before replying. "You can call it what you want. You know the last time I met with you, I was generous enough to let you stay in business. You were weak then, and you're weak now. I fronted you three kilos to help you get back on your feet. Shit! I practically stepped back and let you have the action on the West side. And this is the appreciation I get in return?"

Donta could tell Trey was agitated. "Look Trey, I swear I didn't have nothing to do with this. Being real, I don't appreciate you coming here on my set accusing me of stealing. Now you're trying to embarrass me in front of my crew by telling me what you've done for me. Our business arrangement was simply that, business."

Tim had heard enough. He was ready to get it on. "Donta, this is bullshit and you know it. No matter what you say, he's going to try to pin this shit on you." Trey stared at Tim for a second before taking another puff from his cigar.

"I ain't gon' stand here and let these wanna-be gangsters punk us," Tim said as he continue to stare at Trey.

Trey could sense that Tim had no respect for him as he gave him a cold stare. "I see you finally recruited someone with some heart," Trey stepped closer to Tim while removing the cigar. He blew smoke in Tim's face. "Let me enlighten you, tough guy. Don't speak to me unless I tell you to. Punks like you come a dime a dozen whether you realize that or not. The last time I met with Donta, there was another smart mouth muthafucka just like you. Now unless you want to share coffins with him, I advise you to keep your fuckin' mouth shut!" Trey said standing eye to eye with Tim. As Trey turned to walk away, he was amazed that Tim didn't hold his tongue.

"So I guess because you're the man on the streets, I'm supposed to bow down? Fuck that! I ain't feeling that shit."

Donta knew Tim had gone too far. He tried to intervene before things got worse. Donta did not want this to turn into a gunfight despite feeling a sense of comfort knowing he had the upper hand with shooters in position.

"Hold on, let's take a step back and see if we can work through this. Honestly Trey, I'm telling you I had nothing to do with the jack move this morning. The person who lied to frame me is probably responsible for stealing the kilos."

Trey let Donta's words bounce right off him as he dropped his cigar to the ground and stepped on it. He was thinking about the comments Tim made seconds before Donta spoke. He glanced at Meechi, and nodded his head. "Some niggas just don't know when to keep their mouth shut," Meechi said before pulling out his cell phone to Johnny. "Yo Johnny, Trey needs you to handle our light weight."

"You got it!" Johnny looked through the scope and fired a shot to Tim's temple, killing him instantly. Donta jumped as he witnessed Tim fall to the ground with a bullet hole in his forehead.

"You see Donta, I'm always one step ahead of you. I knew you'd have some shooters in place waiting for me. So, I took the liberty of retiring your men. Now, seeing you only had one loud mouth right-hand man, I hope we can get this shit wrapped up quickly. Otherwise, I'll have to start killing off your entire crew. Now let's take it from the top. What made you think you could get away with robbing me?"

Donta was reluctant to respond. Afraid for his own life, he knew Trey was not going to be satisfied until he admitted robbing him.

"Do you want me to admit to something I didn't do?"

"I just want the truth," Trey responded.

"Trey, like I said before, I had nothing to do with your guys getting robbed."

Trey shook his head in disapproval of Donta's comments. "I guess seeing your boy on the ground with a bullet hole in his head has brought you back to reality. A few minutes ago you were telling me what you didn't appreciate. Now you're acting like a leader with no heart. You know, I believe you're still not feeling me yet." Meechi signaled Johnny to shoot another one of Donta's men.

Craig dropped to the ground as Meechi laughed. "Damn, and another one bites the dust," he commented sarcastically, obviously enjoying every moment of Donta's men being executed.

"Donta, this is getting boring. How many of your men have to die before you confess?"

Almost sure that he was going to die, Donta hoped he could spare a few of men lives. "Trey this ain't solving nothing. You're killing innocent men. If you came to remind me who runs Chicago, fine! I get your point. You are the man. But for the last time, I had nothing to do with your men getting robbed," Trey rubbed his goatee as he thought over Donta's comment.

"You know something, you are absolutely right. This is between you and me." Trey stepped closer to Donta and placed his left arm around Donta's shoulders. He led him away from everyone else. As they walked away, Trey eased his switch blade knife out of his right arm sleeve.

"It's just you and me. Man to man, tell me. Why did you do it?"

At that very moment, Donta knew Trey was totally convinced that he was responsible for robbing him, and the only way out was to kill Trey before he could kill him. He slowly moved his left arm toward his back belt line. "Trey, I know we've had our differences but I swear I had nothing to do with it."

"Okay. I believe you," Trey replied.

Donta felt relieved. He stopped reaching for his gun, thinking that everything was going to be fine.

"Really?" Donta asked.

"Naw," Trey answered just before plunging his switchblade into Donta's chest. Trey pulled the knife from Donta's chest before letting him fall to the ground. Taran, one of Donta's men, saw Trey stab Donta as he was standing several feet away. He immediately reached for his gun. Tony noticed Taran reaching for his gun and pulled out his gun. Trey looked on, noticing both Taran and Tony pulling out their weapons. Tony appeared hesitant to shoot Taran as he fiddled with the safety.

Trey knew Taran had a clear shot at him. He instinctively threw the knife at Taran, knowing if he missed, Taran would kill him for sure. The knife stuck in Taran's neck before he could get a shot off. Trey ran for cover as everyone started shooting. Meechi hid behind his Escalade. He pulled out his cell phone and called for both Johnny and Steve to take out Donta's men. Shots rang down from above. Several of Donta's men start falling. Realizing it was a lost cause, the remaining men decided to give up. Meechi called off the shooters. "Everybody put down your weapons unless you want to die."

Donta's remaining six men dropped their guns and put their hands up as if they were being arrested.

Trey came out of hiding. He appeared furious while approaching Tony. Trey grabbed him by the chin, applying pressure to his lower jaw.

"What the fuck is wrong with you?" Trey asked.

Grimacing in pain, Tony attempted to explain his strange behavior. "I'm sorry, my gun jammed."

In disbelief, he continued to apply pressure to Tony's jaw. "You mean to tell me that after you almost let some fool smoke me, the only thing you can say is you're sorry. Where's your backup piece?"

Struggling to talk, Tony answered. "I got rid of it after popping Brian. I didn't want to get caught up for the heads on it so I ditched it," Tony said as he fell to one knee. The pain from Trey's grip was unbearable. "If you plan to continue working for me, you better have your shit together," Trey replied as he released his grip.

"I'm sorry Trey, I wasn't thinking. I promise it won't happen again," Tony swore as he stood up.

"You damn right it won't happen again! The next time you give someone the opportunity to take a shot at me, I'll kill you and your family, understood?"

Rubbing his cheek bones, Tony glanced over at Meechi. "Yeah, I understand," he replied. Trey turned to face Donta's men. "Listen up. I'm going to say this only once. These are my streets. Donta has been relieved of his duties. If anybody has a problem with this hostile takeover, let it be known." Pausing for a moment, Trey waited for a response. After no one dared to come forth, Trey walked over to Taran's body. He stooped down and pulled his knife out of Taran's neck.

Walking back over to Tony, Trey grabbed his shirt and wiped the blood from the knife onto Tony's shirt. Closing the knife, Trey placed his switchblade inside his Armani jacket pocket. Holding out his hand, Trey added further insult to injury.

"Give me your gun," Tony hesitated, thinking if he gave Trey his gun, he'd probably shoot him with it. Despite his reluctance, he handed him the gun. To his surprise, Trey walked away.

Trey noticed Kerry, Donta's girlfriend brother giving him a hard stare. He approached Kerry.

"That look in your eyes is telling me that you want a piece of me. Am I reading correctly?" Kerry glanced at the gun Trey was holding before responding. "Naw, I'm cool," he responded.

"I see. What's your name?"

"Kerry."

Trey circled Kerry. "Kerry, how would you like to work for me?"

"No thanks. I think I'll pass."

"Have it your way." Trey fired three shots in his chest.

The other five men stood quietly hoping their lives would be spared.

"Being the gentleman that I am, I'm willing to give you guys two options. Either you can accept that Donta is done and work for me, or you can join him. Which will it be?"

The men wasted little time rendering their decision. "We're down," they all replied.

"Smart choice."

Trey uncocked Tony's gun. He walked up to him and shoved the warm barrel into his chest. "You better learn how to work that fuckin' safety. You and Red can put these chumps to work." Trey then approach Meechi. "Let's go. Drop me off at the club. I have to head over to my parents for the family reunion. Hey, why don't you stop by and get a plate?"

Both men climbed into the Escalade. "I might just do that," Meechi replied as they drove away.

CHAPTER 4

THE HIT

Trey was parked across the street from his mom's house. He climbed out of the car and approached his Uncle Tommy who was sitting on the front porch drinking from a half-pint of *E & J.*

"Just the man we've been waiting on. What's up, nephew? I spoke with your wife earlier. You know, she sure is fine!"

Trey could smell the liquor on his uncle's breath. He knew as usual his uncle had too much to drink. Thomas, Kenneth's brother, was the youngest of three brothers. He went into depression the day his brother was buried and had been drinking ever since.

"Hey, don't be making moves on my wife," Trey replied as he hugged him.

"Listen, maybe you should head back inside with me." He grabbed his drunken uncle and guided him back inside.

Trey and Thomas walked out to the backyard. He helped his uncle to a chair before mingling. He turned and saw his Uncle Leonard standing at the barbecue grill doing what he did best. He approached his uncle.

"Giving the meat some extra flavor, I see."

"Yes sir, you know how we do. You can never get enough flavor," Leonard said while pouring a can of beer over the barbecue while flipping over the steaks and hamburgers. He closed the pit to let the meat smoke before smiling and hugging Trey. "It's been awhile since the last time I saw you."

"Yeah, not since the wedding."

Leonard looked Trey over. He couldn't get over how much Trey reminded him of Kenneth. "I heard you've made quite name for yourself on the streets. It's been said that you're this untouchable gangsta."

Trey smiled, feeling proud of himself for stepping into his father's shoes. He had ruled the streets of Chicago for well over a decade now. "Something like that."

"Trey, let me give you a piece of advice. Don't ever think you're untouchable. Check it, you may be the King of the Castle now, but understand that there's always someone on the outside looking for a way to get in."

Trey listened to his uncle's advice despite feeling untouchable. "I'll keep that in mind."

"Fifteen years ago, I had this same conversation with your father. He thought he was the king of the streets. It's so ironic because he said the same exact thing. Trey you do remember what happened to him?"

Trey thought back to that day when Harold shot his father right in front of him. "Yeah, I remember. Do you remember what I did to Harold?"

"Yeah I do," Leonard answered with a smile.

Although he did not approve of his fifteen year old nephew risking his life at the time, he was proud that he was man enough to kill Harold. Something he didn't have the balls to do.

"Son, all I'm saying don't let the streets beat you. By the way, I met your wife. She's a real sweet young lady. She's very intelligent and beautiful. You better hold on to her."

Monica was talking with Leonard's wife Tamika when she noticed Trey standing near the grill talking to his uncle. She wrapped up her conversation with Tamika and headed over. She whispered in Trey's ear after walking up to him.

"We still have some unfinished business to resolve."

Trey gave his uncle a fake grin, not wanting to let on that they were having problems. He turned and kissed Monica on the lips. "I love you too."

Leonard raised the top of the grill to check the meat. "When you get through sweet talking her grab a plate and try some of these rib tips."

Leonard added his last batch of meat after clearing the grill.

"Maybe later," Trey replied as he eased Monica away.

"Where's my son?"

Monica was still laughing at the way Trey ushered her away from his uncle. "Oh, so now you wanna play daddy? He's in your mother's bedroom sleeping. He stayed up half the night. I guess he's getting to be just like his father."

"Listen baby, I'm sorry for hitting you earlier. I promise it will never happen again."

"I know because the next time you raise your hand to me, I promise you won't get a third."

Trey's mother Elaine spotted Trey and Monica together and walked over. "You two are the perfect couple. Your father would be so proud to see how much of a family man you have turned into, God bless his soul."

Monica whispered in Trey's ear, "If she only knew the truth."

Elaine worshipped her Trey. Her only child who reminded her so much of her late husband. Unbeknownst to Trey, his mother often worried about the past reoccurring in the Wilkens' household. "Baby come give your momma a hug." Elaine kissed him on the cheek. "Monica, I have someone I would like you to meet. Crystal is a dear friend of mine. She just loves the way you decorated my home. Crystal would like to talk to you about decorating her nursery."

"Okay, sure. I don't mind talking with her to see what she has in mind."

Elaine grabbed Monica by her arm, practically pulling her away from Trey. "Sweetheart, are your parents joining us today? I haven't seen them since the wedding."

Monica stepped up her pace trying to keep up with Elaine. "Yes, they should be here shortly."

*   *   *   *   *

Candi picked her mother up from the hospital to drive her home. She was immediately disgusted after seeing her brother and his three homies on the front porch playing cards, drinking and smoking. She got out of the car and opened the passenger door to help her mom out of the car. Neither Kelvin nor any of his buddies made a move to assist. Instead, his friends were too busy drooling over Candi's figure. Candi helped her mother up the steps.

"Move fools, let them by!" Kelvin yelled after noticing his friends gawking at his sister while blocking the front door.

Quickly Ronnie and Turk stepped aside. "Hi Ms. Smith," Turk said as he opened the screen door.

"Hi Turk," Ms. Smith responded.

Kelvin lays down his cards. "Y'all bet' not look at my hand," Kelvin said as he followed his mother and sister inside.

"Well, if it ain't Miss California herself. Sis when did you get back?"

"Thursday. Somebody had to pick mom up from the hospital. Apparently you had other commitments. You know, the drinking, smoking and hanging with your thuggish friends."

"Damn, every time you come home you give me shit! Just because you live in L.A. with the stars don't give you the right to think that you're better than us. Sis, don't forget where you came from. Chi-Town baby!"

"Oh, trust I didn't, but obviously you have. You care more about your thuggish ass friends than you do your own mother."

"Both of you need to knock it off!" Ms. Smith demanded.

Candi helped her into the bed. "Mom it's just unacceptable for a grown-ass man to be living off his mother. Instead of getting a job, all he wants to do is hang out and get high."

"Candi just leave him be, okay? Kelvin does just fine by me. Please just let it go!"

"Momma this is bullshit! I'll be glad when she takes her ass back to Cali," Kelvin added.

"Young man you better watch your mouth!" Ms. Smith replied.

Candi decided to bite her tongue for her mother's sake. She rolled her eyes at Kelvin while fluffing the pillows.

"Man I'm outta here," Kelvin said storming out.

He rejoined his friends as they were standing around on the porch shooting the breeze and smoking a blunt. "Man pass me that shit," Kelvin said to Turk.

Turk took another hit before passing the blunt to Kelvin. "Hey K, what's up with your sister?" Turk asked.

"What you mean?" Kelvin replied, giving Turk a hard stare.

"I'm just saying, Candi's hot."

Kelvin took a hit from the blunt. "Nigga first of all, that's my fuckin' sister. Besides that, you're barking up the wrong tree. Candi's sort of spoken for."

"Look K, I know we've smashed a few honey's together but, I'm telling you dog, your sister is wifey material."

"Fool who you think you running game on? Nigga you better kill that noise about my sister before you get drove on. Anyway, Candi only has eyes for one nigga."

"I bet you if I run up on that clown and pull this steel, he'd see it my way and step back," Turk said.

"Yeah Turk, you should do that. Why don't you head over to his club and repeat that shit to Trey," Kelvin replied, chuckling.

"What! K, are you telling me that your sister fucking the King of the Streets?" Turk asked.

"Yo K, that's our ticket to getting paid. Why don't you holla at your sister and see if she could put in a word with Trey?" Ronnie asked.

"I already tried. Trey don't do business like that. You have to prove yourself," Kelvin added.

"Well shit, we got a few capers under our belt," Ronnie replied.

"Yeah, but his game is cocaine and murder. I don't know if we ready to get down like that. Besides, Candi is old news to him. She's been in California for three years. I'm not sure if she still has juice with him."

"K, I don't know about y'all, but I'm down with whatever," Ronnie replied.

"K, I'm down too. We gotta figure out a way to convince Trey to put us on," Turk added.

Kelvin thought for a second as he hit the last of the blunt. "Okay, check it. I got an idea that will definitely convince Trey to put us on."

"Well, what's the plan?" Ronnie asked.

"All right, listen up. If we do this there is no going back," Kelvin replied.

*   *   *   *   *

Terry, Trey's nineteen year old cousin spotted him standing by the refreshment table getting a glass of punch. He walked up to Trey. "What's going on, cuz?"

Trey was sipping on his spiked cup of lemonade and Jack Daniels. "What's up, Shorty? I see Chicago is working for you. When Mom mentioned you were moving out here, I figured in a month you'd be back on a plane to Houston."

Terry, Trey's first cousin, moved to Chicago with his mother six months ago after his parents separated. He learned the hard way that on the streets of Chi-Town, there's no room for weakness and indecisiveness.

"When my mom first left my dad to move here, I hated her for it. We argued for weeks. I finally realized that she was only doing what she felt she had to in order to get peace of mind. Well cuz, it's my turn to do what I got to do. It's time for me to get my hustle on."

Trey couldn't believe his little cousin was growing up. "Hustlin', what do you know about hustlin'?"

"I'm caught up in the game, cuz. It's all about making that paper."

"In six months, Chicago has changed you into a thug? What's up with the new look? I didn't think braids and earrings were your style." Trey laughed, trying to vision his nerdish cousin as a thug.

"It's like this T. These streets are rough. I'm trying to get that cheddar and earn respect from these busters. The old Terry from Texas would probably get chased home every day. Not the new Terry, you see cuz, I ain't taking no shit. I'm trying to raise up," Terry said before shoving a barbecued hot dog down his throat and chasing it with a Sprite.

Trey wasn't convinced that Terry could handle himself on the streets. But he knew if anybody knew he was related to him, they wouldn't fuck with him if they valued their life.

"If you run into any problems you can't handle, you know you can holla at me."

"I feel you. Listen Trey, I know this ain't the perfect place for this but I need a favor. I'm running a little short on ends. I was wondering if you could spot me some work." Trey was caught off guard by Terry's request.

"I don't think so, Shorty. I'm not sold on the new you just yet. Besides, what about Aunt Millie? If she found out, I would never hear the end of it. If you need some ends, I can kick you down a few bills until you get on your feet." Trey reached for his wallet to give Terry some money.

"I'm cool. I don't want a hand out, I just need some work. Come on Trey, we're family. Check it, Mom don't have to know."

Trey swallowed down his drink in disbelief that he was actually considering Terry's request. "All right, Shorty. I will start you out small and see what you can do. Stop by the club later tonight, and I'll get you started. Just remember, these streets are brutal. If you want to gain respect on the streets, you better be ready to pull capers and smoke fools with no hesitation."

"Thanks cuz, I won't let you down," Terry said as he hugged Trey.

"You better not."

Walking away, Trey decided to go check on little Trey. He entered the house and headed through the kitchen toward the hallway corridor. He noticed his uncle Tommy, slumped down on the sofa passed out snoring. He proceeded down the hall to his mother's room. Trey Jr. was sound asleep. His precious little cheeks glowed like a shooting star. Trey was proud to have created something so special. He kissed Junior before fully covering him up with the quilted blanket that was partially covering his tiny body. Exiting the room, Trey headed toward the front door.

Thinking about his father, Trey stepped out of the front door and took a seat on the front steps. The conversation he had with Monica earlier played over and over in his mind. Finally he thought, *Maybe she's right. I think it's time for me to pass the torch.* He knew he had a six month old son that needed all the love and nurturing a family could give him. This helped to confirm his decision. Holding a blunt in hand, Trey pulled out his gold plated lighter with his initials engraved across it and lit the blunt. He took two puffs before Devin, the little boy next door, walked over. He was running toward Trey, aiming his water gun at him.

"Freeze!"

"Little man, what's your name?" Trey asked after exhaling the smoke.
"Devin."

"Devin, how old are you?"

"Ten," he replied as he began choking from the smoke.

"Don't you know you're not supposed to point a gun at an O.G.?" Trey asked as he put out the blunt.

"It's only a water gun. I'm scared of a real gun."

"You should be. Guns are nothing to play with," Trey added as Devin came closer.

"Trey, what's an O.G.?"

"You're too young to learn about the street terminology. When you get old enough, I'll school you," Trey answered, wondering how the kid knew his name.

"All the kids in the neighborhood are always saying how rich you are. When I grow up, I want to be rich just like you."

Devin's comments hit home as Trey could see his son face through Devin's. "Look Devin, doing what I do ain't cool. What's cool is staying in school and getting an education. Don't you want to be an architect or maybe a doctor or something?"

"Not really. They don't drive nice cars and have a lot of money like you do."

"Sure they do. Devin, the most important thing is making yourself and your parents proud of who you are and what you do."

"Trey, you're not either one of them, and you're rich. Why can't I be like you?"

Trey thought for a second before responding to Devin's comments. He felt in his heart that although his mother was proud of his financial success, she would have preferred he'd taken a different path.

"You can't be like me because I say so. Do me a favor, remember what I said little man."

Trey reached into his pocket and pulled out a small roll of cash.

"Here, take this money and stay out of trouble. Buy yourself some ice cream or something."

"Wow! Thanks, Trey."

Devin accepted the twenty dollar bill Trey handed him and ran off to show his mother. "Mommy, look at what he gave me."

Devin's mother stood in the door way smiling at Trey as her son ran up to her. "That was really nice of him. Did you say thank you?"

"Yes ma'am," Devin answered.

"Come on baby, let's go inside," Devin's mother suggest after taking a brief second to undress Trey with her eyes.

Trey would never admit it but since becoming a father, the one thing he feared more than anything was not being around to watch his son grow up. He relit his blunt and took a few puffs as he continued thinking about how different his life could have been if his dad was still alive.

Trey looked up as he heard tires squealing from the dark blue four-door Chevy Trailblazer with 22's. He immediately recognized the approaching SUV after reading the license plate which read BLAZING. As the truck slightly slowed down, Trey spotted Derek, one of his entourage members, pointing an AK 47 at him. Trey dropped the blunt, and reach for his gun as he jumped up and bailed for cover.

Squeezing the trigger, Derek fired a round off. Trey was hit in the chest but continued to fire back. As Trey dropped to the ground, Terrell punched the accelerator and sped off. Trey was lying on his mother's lawn motionless with five bullet holes in his Armani suit. His mind traveled back to happier moments in his childhood with his father. Visions flash in and out as Kenneth taught Trey how to ride a bike and then how to hit the punching bag. His memory skipped ahead to the day his father got shot by Harold. The vision vanished as Trey opened his eyes. In pain, Trey struggled to sit up as everyone from the reunion started to gather around. He touched the bulletproof vest thinking if it wasn't for the business he had to settle right before coming to the reunion, he would not have been wearing the vest and would be pushing up daisies.

Monica made her way through the crowd. She saw Trey lying on the lawn and rushed to his side. "Trey, are you okay?"

"I'm fine. Those fools missed me."

Elaine rushed through the crowd. "My baby, are you alright? We heard gunshots."

Trey picked himself and his gun up off the grass. Trey could read Monica's *I told you so* expression.

"I'm okay. Just some player haters trying to make a name for themselves," he answered as she noticed the bullet holes in his Armani jacket.

"Oh my God!"

"Mom, don't worry, I'm fine."

Everyone starts heading back to the party. Trey hugged his mother to ensure her he was okay.

"I have to take care of this. I'll see you later," Trey said as he released her and started toward his car.

"Trey, no! Please don't do anything foolish. Trey, you listen to me. Leave it be. If you go looking for trouble, you might get yourself killed. Monica, please talk some sense into your husband."

Monica was just as concerned as Elaine. She knew that Trey was going after the guys that tried to kill him, no matter what anyone said.

"Trey, don't do this. Please listen to your mother. You can't go chasing trouble."

Determined to twist their cap back, Trey climbed in his car ignoring his mother and Monica. Trey felt betrayed and disrespected by the fact that his own men came to his mother's home and attempted to kill him in front of his family. As Trey drove off, Monica stood on the edge of the curb watching his car until it was out of site. She closed her eyes and prayed to God that her husband would return.

CHAPTER 5

VENGEANCE IS MINE

An hour later, Derek and Terrell made their way over to Terrell's house. Shortly after parking, they climbed out of the car, leaving the radio playing. They were listening to The Realist's single *My Block* with their guns in hand celebrating killing Trey.

"Yeah, we got his ass! Man, everybody is going to be on our tip for killing Trey."

"Who would have thought that Trey would get smoked by his own crew?"

"Yo, he never saw that one coming. Fire up that blunt."

*   *   *   *   *

Trey had nothing but vengeance in his heart. He thought about what he was going to do to both men when he caught up with them. He queued up one of his favorite songs 2PAC's *When We Ride On Our Enemies.* He turned up the song as he turned down Terrell's street. Trey slowed down as he spotted Terrell and Derek standing in the street dancing.

Derek noticed the car slowly approaching with high beams on. "I wish that fool would turn off those high beams."

"Ain't that Trey's car?"

Trey stopped approximately fifty feet away. He climbed out with gun in hand. Derek and Terrell were in disbelief.

"It can't be. You're dead! We killed you!"

Trey aimed his gun at them while savoring the moment. Firing several shots, Trey hit both Derek and Terrell as they traded gunfire with him. Their nervousness caused them both to miss their mark. Lying in the middle of the street in pain, Derek and Terrell both tried to reason with Trey as he walked up to them. Terrell was shot in the chest and right arm. He managed to turn himself over. He tried to reach his gun which was just a few feet away. Trey watched as Terrell continued to crawl toward his gun. Once he finally reached it, Trey stepped on his hand and shot him in the back of his head, killing him instantly.

Derek laid helpless after being shot in the knee. He witnessed Trey kill Terrell and knew he was next.

"Trey, please don't kill me," he begged.

Trey stood over Derek pointing his gun at his face. He could clearly see the anger in Trey's eyes. "That depends on the answer you give me. Who put you up to this?"

Hoping it would save his life, Derek wasted little time spilling the beans.

"It was Meechi. He setup the whole thing. Meechi paid Terrell and me to kill you. He was also the one behind the robbery this morning. He wanted you to think Donta pulled the heist so you would kill him. He figured with both of you out the way, he could take over. Trey, he made us do it."

Trey's stone-faced expression sent chills down Terrell's spine. Trey was stunned at what he heard. He originally thought Donta's twin brother Shante' was behind the caper.

"So, he did, huh? If this is true, why didn't you both come to me?"

"Trey you got to believe me, he said if we didn't do it he would kill our family. I wanted to tell you, but I was afraid that you wouldn't believe us."

"Okay, I understand. I believe you," Trey said before lowering his gun and turning to walk away.

Derek lets out a sigh in relief after Trey spared his life.

"Thank you Lord."

Trey turned around and faced Derek. "I wouldn't thank him just yet. I said I believe you, but I never said anything about letting you live."

Aiming his gun at Derek, Trey fired two shots hitting him in the chest, killing him.

Looking down at Derek, Trey could feel a set of eyes piercing over him. He looked up and noticed Perry watching him. Perry, the neighborhood dope fiend who lived three houses down from Terrell, was taking out the trash when he heard the gunshots. Perry fell over the trash cans not sure where the shots were coming from. Seconds later, he gathered himself and looked up the street and saw Trey standing in the middle of the street with gun in hand. He immediately recognized Trey, figuring he picked the wrong time to empty the trash. Paranoid, Perry's heart was pounding. He quickly eased his way up to his front door. Trey stared Perry down for a few seconds before turning to head back to his car. He climbed into his vehicle and drove away.

*   *   *   *   *

Perry looked around after waiting a few minutes to make sure it was safe to investigate. He was momentarily at odds with himself in trying to decide whether or not to check the guys for dope. He made up his mind and eased down the street. He pulled Terrell's wallet out of his back pocket and opened it. Perry smiled as he counted the money which totaled two hundred and fifty dollars. He put the wallet back in Terrell's pocket, then moved over to Derek's body. As he bent down to check his pockets, several squad cars swooped down on him.

Officers O'Neil and Jackson jumped out the squad car and pointed their guns at Perry. "Don't move!"

Minutes later, Sergeant Turner drove up and witnessed the officers on the scene handcuffing Perry. He climbed out his vehicle and started toward them.

"Who do we have this time?" Sgt. Turner, a tall bald Caucasian with a chip on his shoulder, asked.

"Two male casualties, Derek Johnson, age 26 and Terrell Wallace, age 28. Mr. Wallace lives here at 3968 Augusta," Officer Billups responded after shoving Perry into the back of his squad car. "We've got two black males lying in the middle of the street with their guns next to them. Could be a drug deal gone sour," Sgt. Turner added.

"That's a good possibility. Both have a rap sheet a mile long."

"Who made the 911 call?"

"Mrs. Burns, an elderly lady down the street. She stated she heard gun shots."

"I'm getting tired of dead bodies popping up all over the city. Who's the clown in your car?"

"When Officers O'Neil and Jackson arrived on the scene, they found this junkie going through the stiff's pockets. His name is Perry Taylor, age 31. He lives at 3961 Augusta, three houses down from one of the stiffs. I'm sure he knows something but, he's not talking."

"You know the drill. Arrest him and book 'em for suspicion of two counts of murder. We'll see if he changes his mind and decides to talk."

CHAPTER 6

IT'S ON

Meechi, Red and Tony were sitting in Trey's private section watching 314 perform. Meechi glanced around the club with a smile thinking, *all this is mine.* Meechi felt like he was on top of the world now that Trey was out of the way. Shatina was standing near the bar when she spotted the three of them sharing laughs in the restricted section. She walked over to the table.

"Where's Trey?"

"Good question," Red answered, laughing as if she missed the punch line.

"Shatina, bring me a bottle of Dom P," Meechi requested.

"Does Trey know you guys are using his restricted section?" Shatina asked, sensing something was wrong.

"What difference does it make? Just bring me the damn bottle of champagne."

"Get it yourself," Shatina said as she turned to walk away.

Meechi jumped out of his seat and grabbed her by the arm. "I'm tired of your smart-ass mouth. Just because you're fucking the boss don't mean you're running shit."

"Let go of my arm. You're hurting me!"

"If you know what's good for you, you'll bring me that bottle of champagne and stop giving me lip." Meechi kissed Shatina on the cheek before releasing her arm.

"Sure, I'll bring you your bottle of champagne. But just remember, when Trey gets here, you're going to wish you hadn't asked for it."

The three of them laughed as she walked away. "Did you hear her? When Trey gets here I'm going to wish I hadn't ordered champagne? What difference would it make to him considering he's dead?"

Trey was standing behind them. He clearly heard Meechi's comment.

"What give you that idea?"

The three men quickly turned around. They were speechless. Tony was sipping on some cognac and almost choked to death on one of the ice cubes.

"Trey, what are you doing here?"

Meechi was stunned to see Trey after getting confirmation from Tony earlier that Trey was dead.

"This is my club, remember? What's wrong fellas? Y'all look as if you've just seen a ghost?"

Tony and Red were horrified. Despite Trey's suave and mellow appearance, they knew all so well beneath that relaxed persona lay a cold blooded killer. They'd witness first-hand how ruthless Trey could be over the years. This would surely push him over the edge.

"Trey, no disrespect intended. It's just that it's all over the streets that you got gunned down in front of your mother's house earlier."

Shatina returned with Meechi's bottle of Dom Perignon. "Hi Trey, I told them they weren't supposed to be at your restricted section, but they all just laughed."

"Oh really?" Trey stared at the three men without speaking. Looking into each one of their eyes, he could see the fear. As Trey eyes shifted to Meechi, he wanted to pull out his gun and blowout his brains all over the table right then and there. Fortunately, he thought better of it.

Trey pulled the bottle of champagne out of the ice bucket Shatina was holding to see what they ordered. "So, is this what the celebration is all about? I'm supposed to be dead. You're all sitting in my off limits section, ordering what, Dom Perignon. I see you spared no expense. Instead of turning corners trying to find my killer, you three are here having drinks on me."

Meechi tried not to panic. He wondered how much of their conversation Trey actually overheard.

"Trey, it ain't like that. We were celebrating how far we have come with you. We started as smalltime hustlers and look at us now, fucking entrepreneurs. We've been balling out of control."

Trey listened to Meechi feed him a line of bullshit while he thought to himself just how much he was going to enjoy giving the three of them actually what they deserved.

"That sounds better. 'Cause I would hate to think my crew would actually be in my club, celebrating my death."

Trey's comments left the three men with an awkward look on their face. Sitting in silence, Tony tried to avoid eye contact with Trey. Remembering what Trey said to him earlier, he started to second guess his decision to partner up with Meechi. Red too was becoming skeptical about Meechi's scheme but knew it was too late to turn back. Shatina could feel the tension between Trey and Meechi as she stood next to Trey. Finally, Trey broke his silence.

"Meechi, I'm expecting my cousin Terry to stop by the club. When he gets here send him back to my office."

"No problem."

Trey walked away from the table and headed to his office. Meechi looked up at Shatina after noticing she was still standing at the table with a smirk on her face.

"What! Why are you still here?"

"I knew you bums were just talking shit. Meechi, I hope you enjoy your champagne because you're going to need it to wash down all the ass you just ate." Shatina dropped the ice bucket with the bottle of champagne on the table and walked away laughing.

"Damn! Tony what the fuck is going on? I thought you said Terrell and Derek both told you they killed him?" Meechi asked while knocking the wine glasses off the table in frustration.

"Shit! I don't know. I'm just as surprised as you. That's what they told me."

"Well he don't look dead to me. Meechi, I told you we couldn't count on those fools," Red added before standing up and walking away from the table.

"Tony, get those clowns on the phone now and find out what the fuck happened," Meechi yelled.

*   *   *   *   *

Terry entered the club. He looked around before noticing Meechi at a table by himself. He made his way through the crowd and approached him.

"Meechi, what's up? Where's Trey?"

Red rejoined Meechi as he was returning from the restroom, and Tony was making his way back to the table as well.

"Little man, how did you get in here? You ain't twenty one."

"Why are you sweating me, cuz? I walked in just like you did."

Red stepped closer to Terry while Tony took a seat at the table. "Look young buck, you ain't no gangsta. I see you've gotten some heart you little punk. Don't think just because you're Trey's cousin, I won't kick your ass."

Terry shoved Red into the table. "You don't want none of this cuz."

"Red, chill, Terry follow me. Trey is waiting on you," Meechi said, jumping between the two of them before deciding to take Terry to Trey's office.

Moments later, Meechi returned to the table giving Red an unimpressed stare.

"What the fuck was that?" As Red was about to speak, Meechi cut him off.

"Don't answer. Don't say a fuckin' word! Man, I need a drink. Hey, bring me some clean glasses after you finish cleaning that shit up," Meechi demanded as he watched the bartender sweep up the broken glass.

Tony laid his phone on the table after unsuccessfully having any luck reaching Terrell and Derek. "No one has seen or heard from them. I called both of their cell phones but got no answer."

"We've got to finish the job we started," Meechi added as he started contemplating his next move.

*   *   *   *   *

An hour later, Candi, Trey's ex-girlfriend, entered the club. Her silky, long hair, pretty brown complexion and luscious figure turned heads immediately. As she approached the bar, she spotted Meechi sitting in the back of the club.

"How's it going, stranger?"

Meechi glanced at her before doing a double take. "Damn! Look at you. California definitely agrees with you." Meechi hugged her after checking out her shape.

"So where is that good looking boss of yours?"

"You mean Trey? He's in the back. Here, have a seat. What brought you back to Chicago? You finally figured your life would never be complete without me?"

Candi smiled as Meechi poured her a drink. "You wish. I'm here visiting my mother."

"How long have you been here?"

"I flew in Thursday afternoon."

"What, you mean to tell me you've been here for two days and just now stopping in to see me?"

"Something like that. So Meechi, how are you?"

"I'm cool. I could be doing a lot better if you would have taken me up on my offer instead of leaving town."

Candi shook her head while laughing in amazement. "You never stop talking shit, do you?"

"I'll say whatever necessary to get with you baby."

"Meechi, we've been through this. You are Trey's friend. How can you even think that I would consider dating you?"

Meechi stared at Candi thinking how much he would give to fuck her. He got a hard-on just thinking about getting between her legs. The red dress clinging to her body didn't make it any better.

"I know. You've sung this song before. Things are a lot different now. Trey is married, but I'm not. Hell, I'm ready for you to have my baby."

Candi blushed, though not pleased to hear that Trey was taken. "Can we change the subject? I see the club is doing great."

"Yeah, except my next act just cancelled on me because she lost her voice. You know, I just had a thought..."

"What?" Candi asked curiously.

"How would you like to fill in for me as the next act? I'm sure you still have that great singing voice."

Candi thought for a second thinking how exciting it would be to perform again after a three year hiatus. Those were the happiest days of her life. Candi reminisced back to when she last performed. She was in love. Trey held her hand as he stood on the stage introducing her to the crowd.

"Candi! Will you do it?"

"I don't know about this Meechi. It's been a while since I've sung in front of an audience."

"Candi, come on. You'll be fine." Meechi jumped out of his chair and pulled Candi to the stage.

"What about Trey?"

"I'll let him know you're here. Now stop stalling and let's do this."

Meechi walked onto the stage and picked up the microphone. "Tonight, we have a very special guest. She's a dear friend of mine. Please put your hands together for Candi!"

Candi stepped onto the stage and approached the band. She instructed them of her music arrangement. Meechi handed her the microphone and left the stage. She was center staged as the band started playing. Candi decided to sing one of her favorite songs she used to perform in the club. She glanced around the club for a second.

"Tonight, I will take you all back. Because I know every woman in here has experienced real love in their life. The name of my song is titled *Reminisce*."

Trey walked out of his office with Terry after getting word that Candi was waiting to see him. He saw her on stage and made his way through the crowd. Candi noticed Trey edging closer to the stage. She smiled and continued to sing, hoping he would realize the song was about the two of them.

After finishing the song, Candi took a standing ovation. Everyone whistled and clapped in appreciation. She exited the stage and approached Trey.

"I see you finally decided to grace me with your presence."

"I could say the same about you," Trey replied.

"You know me, I just can't stay away. Trey Wilkens, you were the love of my life. It has taken me three years to get over you. Seeing you now, I'm still not sure that I have."

Trey paused momentarily, thinking about how good it would be to have Candi in his life again. Then he thought about the way their relationship ended.

"Candi, baby I'm sorry about the way things ended between us. At the time, I wasn't ready for marriage and a family."

"Well, it seems as if something or someone changed that. So is it true, are you married?"

Trey motioned for Candi to follow him as he grabbed her by the hand and led her over to his table.

"I guess you've been talking to Meechi. It's true. I'm married, and I have a son."

"How old is he?"

"Six months," Trey replied.

"Did you name him after you?"

"Yeah, he's a junior."

Candi tried to hide the hurt, but it was obvious that she wished she could trade places with Monica.

"Trey, what did she have to offer you that you obviously felt you couldn't get from me?"

"Candi, this is nothing personal. I did love you. You know me, I just didn't want a commitment. After a few months went by without hearing from you, I realized that I let the best thing that ever happened to me slip away. Monica came along and a year later, she put me in the same position you did. She caught me at a vulnerable time. I didn't want to make the same mistake twice, so I married her."

Shatina noticed Trey and Candi sitting together at his table. She knew her place with Trey, but always hoped that one day he would leave Monica and they could be together. Seeing the two of them together made her feel like Candi was invading her territory. She wasn't having that. She moseyed over to the table.

"Trey, can I get you anything to drink?"

"Yes, bring me A Glass Full of Sin."

Shatina glared at Candi as if she wanted to cut her throat. She turned to walk away. "Miss, I'll take an Amaretto Sour."

"Sure, whatever," Shatina responded as she glanced back, rolling her eyes at Candi before walking away.

Candi laughed off Shatina's rudeness, figuring it must had something to do with her being with Trey.

"Well, she sure has great people skills."

"Don't pay her any attention."

"I take it she must be another one of your conquests."

"I wouldn't say that."

"I beg to differ."

Shatina returned with their drinks. She placed Trey's drink in front of him. Turning to Candi, she dropped her drink on the table, spilling a touch of it on the table. Shatina tossed Candi a napkin and started to walk off. Trey had seen enough.

"Shatina, what the fuck is your problem? Get her a new drink, wipe that shit up and apologize."

Not wanting to risk pissing him off further, Shatina wiped the liquor up off the table. "I'm sorry. Let me get you a new drink."

"I'm fine. I'll keep this one."

Shatina left the table, embarrassed and hurt.

"I think you hurt her feelings," Candi suggested to Trey after taking a sip of the drink.

"She'll get over it."

"So what's A Glass Full of Sin?"

"It's one of the new drinks I created. It has a mixture of Hennessy, Gin, Ciroc, Tequila and a splash of lemon juice with two cherries, on the rocks."

"It sounds really intriguing, but I will stick with my norm. Well, I wish you and your wife the best. I hope that you're happy."

"Monica's a great woman. She's just too damn demanding."

Candi chuckled figuring it was Trey that had the problem with commitment. "Let me guess. She wants you to come home every night, show her some affection, and be more of a father figure to your son."

Trey swallowed down his drink. He smiled, impressed at how accurately Candi captured his family issues.

"Damn, do you have a crystal ball in that purse of yours?"

"I know you. You love your freedom. Her demands are no different from any woman in a committed relationship. Trey, things are a lot different now. You have a wife and son. It's going to takes a lot of sacrifice to make it work."

"Thanks for the advice, Oprah. I'll keep it in mind."

Candi knew it was wrong in her heart to feel this way, but she was happy to hear he was having marital issues. This meant there was a chance for her to possibly work her way back into his heart.

"Trey, it doesn't sound as if you're taking this seriously."

"I guess I better. Monica threatened to leave me if I don't change into this fuckin' choir boy."

Candi laughed figuring Trey was over dramatizing the situation. "It sounds to me that you don't want to change?"

Trey thought for a second before responding. He thought about how Meechi tried to kill him and what he had in store for him. "You know me. I've got to have my independence. Besides, I've got some unfinished business with someone."

"Trey, I don't mean to sound dramatic but, your business and independence may cause you to lose her. Is that what you really want?"

Trey reached across the table to touch her hand. "If I do, will you be there for me?"

"Always," she responded as she leaned across the table and planted a kiss on his cheek.

"I'm glad you're back. By the way, you never said what brought you here."

Trey's question reminded her that she had to go back to the pharmacy to pick up her mother's prescription. "I'm here visiting my mother. She had foot surgery two days ago. I flew in to help her out for a couple of days."

"I'm sorry to hear that. Let me know if there's anything I can do."

"Okay, I will."

"So, you're staying with your mom?"

"Heavens no, my brother has too much drama going on there. You know, the girls and drugs. I rented a room."

"Yeah, it's time for his grown ass to get his own place," Trey replied.

"I tried to get mom to come stay with me at the hotel, but she wants to sleep in her own bed."

"Your mom don't want to leave Kelvin in that house alone."

"Truthfully, I don't blame her." Candi decided to move in for the kill before losing her nerve. "Well Trey, I better get going. Listen, since you don't plan on changing into this one woman man overnight, I was hoping that you wouldn't mind stopping by later for a drink."

"I might just take you up on that offer."

Candi and Trey both stood from the table. She walked up to Trey and slammed a passionate kiss on him. Candi opened Trey's hand and gave him her hotel room key. "I'm pretty sure you'll still enjoy the way my candy tastes. I'm staying at the Embassy Suites downtown. My flight leaves tomorrow evening at 6pm. Come by and give me a reason to stay."

Meechi was sitting at the bar watching as Candi exited the club. He approached Trey. "Candi is still hot. I was talking to her earlier. She still has a thing for you."

"I will always care about Candi, but my future is with Monica," Trey added as he stared at the room key.

CHAPTER 7

LET'S TALK

Perry sat in the interrogation room still wearing handcuffs. Sergeant Turner entered with a tall man in a gray suit and matching brim. The tall officer was holding a manila folder. He dropped it on the table and sat back and sipped on his coffee. He sat the cup down on the table in front of Perry.

"Perry, let me take those handcuffs off for you," Sgt. Turner suggested as he pulled out his key and unlocked the cuffs. He placed the cuffs down on the table and took a seat directly across from Perry.

"Perry, I'm Sgt. Richard Turner and this is Lieutenant William Dawson. We would like to give you the opportunity to tell us what happened to the two guys we found you robbing."

"From the looks of things they were killed," Perry replied as he rubbed his left wrist. "Why don't you try telling us something we don't know?"

"I don't know what you expect me to say. Look, I didn't kill those guys."

"When my officers arrived on the scene, they found you going through their pockets. If you didn't kill them, why were you going through their pockets?"

"I figured since they were both dead, the money wasn't going to do them any good."

Lt. Dawson removed his hat and placed it on the table. "Look, no more games. You say you didn't kill them, but you expect me to believe you stumbled upon the two dead men and suddenly decided to rob them?"

"That's pretty much what happened."

Sgt. Turner was quickly losing patience with Perry. "Okay, cut the shit right now. Tell us where you hid the murder weapon and why you did it?"

"I told you cop, I didn't kill no one. Now, I'm not saying another word until my lawyer gets here. I know my rights."

Sgt. Turner jumped out of his chair and grabbed Perry by his shirt, hoping to rattle him. "Don't toy with us junkie. I've checked you out. You're on six months of probation for breaking and entering. Your rap sheet is a mile long, so cut the shit! I could pin these murders on you easily and not give it a second thought. Now you're going to tell us what you know, or I'll lock your ass up and throw away the key!"

Perry knew if he talked, Trey would come after him. He also knew if he didn't talk, he would probably spend the rest of his life in prison for murders he didn't commit. Knowing his back was up against the wall, he had no choice but to come clean.

"Okay look, I'm no rat, but I did see who shot them." Sgt. Turner released his grip from Perry's shirt.

"Finally, we're getting somewhere."

"Give me a name," Lt. Dawson said.

Perry hesitated for a moment before coming clean. "This guy is big trouble. The man you're looking for drives a blue two-door vehicle. The license plate reads *HUSTLIN*."

Lt. Dawson opened the folder which contained two photos inside. "Perry, was one of these guys the shooter?"

Perry pointed to the photo on the left.

"Are you sure?" Sgt. Turner asked.

"Positive. That's him."

"That's Trey Wilkens. We've been investigating his organization for
years. I've finally got him now."

"Okay well, I guess that clears me, right?"

"Perry, you have no idea how big this arrest and conviction will be for
our Precinct. Trey is one of the largest cocaine distributors in the
Midwest."

"I guess this must be your lucky day."

"Until now, we could never get anything solid on him that would stick.
With your testimony, we can put him away for a long time. He's
probably the reason for the other eight bodies we found this morning."

"Eight bodies!" Perry knew he had made a huge mistake and wanted
no part of fingering Trey. "No way, I'm sorry that you and this guy
have history, but I did my part. I gave you the shooter so I should be
free to go, right?"

"Son, unfortunately, it's not that simple. We will place you under
protective custody until the trial is over."

"What trial? I thought I was just here to tell you what happened. Look
man, I gave you the killer. I'm not testifying against no one, especially
a killer of his caliber. Ten bodies is a lot of killing for one man."

Lt. Dawson leaned over the table, getting in Perry's face.

"Son, this ain't multiple choice. You don't have a choice in this. Either
you agree to testify, or I will tell Trey personally that you came to us
and identified him as the shooter. I'd like to see how long you last on
the streets." Both Sgt. Turner and Lt. Dawson stepped away from the
table heading towards the door.

"Wait a minute, this ain't right. This is blackmail!" Perry yelled,
knowing if Trey knew he snitched, he would be dead for sure.

"Son, this is law enforcement," Lt. Dawson answered as both men exited the interrogation room.

*   *   *   *   *

Trey just finished counting the last of his money with an automatic money counter. He placed the stacks of fifty and hundred dollar bills into the safe and closed it as Meechi entered.

"Trey, the cops are here. I think you better come check this out."

"I'll be right out." Trey placed the picture of his father back in front of the safe then headed out into the club area. He saw Meechi talking to Sgt. Turner as he approached.

"Officers, what can I do for you?"

"Trey Wilkens, we have a warrant for your arrest and a warrant to search the premises. You are under arrest for the murders of Derek Johnson and Terrell Wallace," Sgt. Turner replied as he flashed the warrant.

Officer Derek Graves, a short, freckle faced white male in his mid-twenties hesitated before cuffing Trey. Derek preferred it had been anyone else besides himself. He knew for years Sgt. Turner had tried to put Trey away since the killing of his son at the club. Trey would always make someone pay. He could only hope that Trey would not seek vengeance on him and his family. Sgt. Turner started back towards Trey's office. He opened the door and proceeded to Trey's desk. He opened drawer after drawer until he found a nickel-plated .380 inside a small black leather gun case.

"Did you find something?" asked Officer Graves as he joined him.

"Hopefully, he better pray this ain't the murder weapon," Sgt. Turner answered as he continued to search throughout the office.

Moments later, Sgt. Turner and Officer Graves rejoined Trey and the other officers as they waited their return. He was carrying the black gun case.

"Trey, I hope you got a license to carry this firearm. If you don't, I promise you I'm going to toss you in jail and shut this club down for having an illegal firearm on the premises."

As usual, Trey was hard to read. He refused to answer as he gave Sgt. Turner a cold stare.

"Take this clown out of here," Sgt. Turner ordered the officers as they all marched toward the exit.

Meechi and Red looked on as the officers escorted Trey out of the club to the waiting squad car.

"That explains why we couldn't reach them. They're dead."

"That's what those dumb mutha-fuckas get. They were supposed to kill him, not get killed."

"You think they told Trey we paid them to kill him?"

"Maybe. Honestly I really don't give a fuck. Besides, if they had told him, we would be dead already."

"Good point. At least he'll be behind bars for a minute."

"I doubt it. He'll be out in a couple hours. Don't worry, this should give us enough time to plan our next move."

* * * * *

Sgt. Turner and three fellow officers escorted Trey to his assigned cell. Several inmates recognized Trey as he walks past their cell.

"Trey, what's up, peoples? Can I roll with you when I get out?" One of the inmates asked as he and his cellmate watched Trey be escorted past their cell.

"Who is he?" asked Inmate Two.

"Man, are you kidding me? Everybody knows Trey Wilkens? Everybody calls him the King of the Streets. Man he is pushing major weight. He's got Chicago on lock dirty. I hear he takes care of his crew, but if you cross him, you'd better leave the country."

"Straight, he's rolling like that?"

"Check it. Six months ago one of his runners stole two kilos from him. Trey went to his house and made his family watch while he cut dude up in pieces. He dared any of his family to talk to the police. You best believe, nobody said a word."

"Damn! Sounds like my man is sadistic and has major juice."

"You think. His father was Kenneth Wilkens. You know the story. This dude name Harold shot the Chicago Drug Lord in front of his son and became the new King of the Streets. Several months later, the fifteen year old kid took out Harold and his right hand man."

"Yeah, I remember that, but I thought that was just a street myth."

"Nope, that fifteen-year-old kid is him. Dude, I'm telling you, I hear he even got some cops on his payroll."

"Yeah, but yet he's in here with us?"

"Sgt. Turner is as usual trying to impress the new Lieutenant. I bet you he'll be out in an hour."

"I wouldn't want to fuck with him," Inmate Two added as they continued to watch the officers escort Trey to his cell.

Finally, the procession stopped. Sgt. Turner smiled as he looked at Trey. He figured this time he had enough evidence to put Trey away for good. "Mr. Wilkens, until you decide to talk this will be your new home. If I was you, I'd get use to calling it home sweet home. I've got your ass this time, Mr. Untouchable," Sgt. Turner commented as he opened the cell door.

Trey enters the cell. His cool, relaxed expression made Sgt. Turner a little uneasy. "You know, Richie, you just don't know when to quit do you? For years you've been trying to get something on me. It's not my fault because your bitch-ass son got himself popped in front of my club."

Sgt. Turner tried to hide the hurt from Trey's comment. "One trip down memory lane deserves another. I see you are following your father's footsteps. I wonder how long it'll be before you get murdered by your own crew just like he did." Trey stared without responding, knowing his crew was indeed trying to kill him.

"What's the matter Trey, did I hit a nerve?"

"I must admit, your persistence impress me. Although I must say, you're starting to irritate me. Give it up, your son is dead. Richie, you can't destroy me. You see, I'm just beginning to floss. It's going to take a lot more than some smalltime sergeant to take away my era of dominance. If you haven't learned by now, you never will."

"That's big talk considering you're standing inside my jail cell."

Trey laughed off Sgt. Turner comments. "We've been here and done this before. Like many times before, I always win. Let me school you, Richie. You and I play by a different set of rules. You can only go so far, while me, there's no limit to what I might do."

Trey's words were obviously starting to get to Sgt. Turner. He turned and motioned to walk away.

"Petty cops like you don't realize how quickly shit can happen. You of all people should know."

Trey comment stopped Sgt. Turner in his tracks before he slowly turned to hear Trey continue. "If I was you, I'd keep a close eye on that pretty daughter of yours. After all, she's the only child you have left."

Sgt. Turner had heard enough. Charging Trey, he grabbed him by the jacket and shoved him against the wall. "You son of a bitch! If you touch my daughter, I'll kill you!"

"Oh, I see I got your attention," Trey responded.

Other officers began immediately rushing into the cell attempting to separate the two men.

"Sgt. Turner, let him go!" Officer Billups requested as he and the other officers shoved Sgt. Turner out of the cell.

"You saw that, police brutality!" Trey said to Officer Billups.

"I didn't see anything," he answered as he closed and locked the cell.

"Richard, don't let him get to you. You have him right where you want him," Officer Billups commented as he pats Sgt. Turner on the shoulder.

"Is that what you think? That's easy for you to say. He didn't threaten your daughter's life."

Sgt. Turner turned and walked away knowing that he had to take Trey's threat very seriously. Officer Billups stood in front of Trey's cell staring at him as the rest of the officers followed Sgt. Turner.

"Hey cop, when do I get my phone call?"

Officer Billups flipped him off before walking away.

*   *   *   *   *

Meechi was sitting at Trey's desk, looking at the picture of Trey, Monica and Trey Jr. He gently rubbed the picture while lusting after Monica. *Soon, everything will be mine, including your fine ass*, he thought to himself as he held the picture. The ring of his cellphone startled him from his daydream.

"Hello?" he answered.

"Meechi, call Walter. Tell Walter I need him to get downtown as soon as possible. One more thing, I have five hundred thousand in the safe. Open the safe, and take out three hundred and fifty thousand and take it to him. Tell him to bring the money with him."

"I don't know the combination to the safe," Meechi said. *Trey is up to something. Why would he tell me how much money was in the safe.*

"It's six to the left, two to the right and eight to the left."

"Why do you need all this money? You don't even know how much your bail will be?"

"Just do what I asked. Take him the money and tell him to get his ass down here!"

"Whatever you say boss," he said right before Trey slammed down the phone, ending their call.

Meechi walked over to the safe to try the combination. It opened on the first try, and Meechi just stared at all the money. Wondering should he do what Trey asked, Meechi started pulling out the money. The hundred dollar bills were bundled together and labeled $10,000 for each stack he removed from the safe. *Yeah, I'll do what you ask for now until I kill your ass,* Meechi thought to himself as he continued to count each stack he removed until it totaled of $350,000.

CHAPTER 8

CASH RULES

Around six am the next morning, Officer Billups escorted Trey into the interrogation room, shoving him toward the table. Sgt. Turner and Lt. Dawson were already in the room waiting.

"Have a seat, Mr. Wilkens. I'm Lt. Dawson. I'm going to get straight to the point. Why did you kill Derek Johnson and Terrell Wallace? Didn't they work for you?"

Trey sat in his chair still handcuffed. He looked at both, but did not respond. "Answer the question."

"I don't know what you're talking about."

"You know exactly what we're talking about," Sgt. Turner replied.

"Excuse me sir. His lawyer is here," Officer Billups said, entering the room.

"Bring him in. This should be a real treat," Sgt. Turner responded, clearly agitated.

The three of them sat quietly waiting as Walter Ashcroft, Trey's Jewish lawyer, entered the room holding a leather black briefcase. Ashcroft was in his mid-thirties. He had soft black naturally curly hair. He was wearing an expensive blue Versace suit with flashy prescription glasses and shiny black Versace dress shoes.

"Good morning, gentlemen. Is it possible for me to have a few minutes alone with my client before we start?"

Sgt. Turner smiled, figuring he had Trey's back against the wall. "Sure, take all the time you need. He's not going anywhere."

Sgt. Turner, Lt. Dawson, and Officer Billups all left the room.

"You're late. What the hell happened to you? You were supposed to be here last night."

"I'm sorry I didn't make it. My wife went into labor before Meechi called last night. I didn't get the message until early this morning."

"Forgive me for not being in a congratulating mood. I spent the night in jail, and I don't intend on spending another night here."

"Trey, why did you insist on me bringing this money down here?" Trey glanced at the briefcase. "I want you to convince them to drop all the charges against me."

"Damn it, Trey! They have you for two counts of murder. How can I possibly get them to drop that?"

Trey thought for a second before responding. "You know, Walter, I'm sure there are a lot of other attorneys that would love to get the money that I pay you. I pay you a lot of money for your services, more than your standard fees because I expect certain things. One of the things I expect is cooperation. If I'm in jail and not on the streets making money, then we have a problem. Do you know why, Walter? Because this means I'm paying my lawyer for services he's not providing. This upsets me. I suggest you get on your fuckin' J-O-B and get me the fuck out of here!"

"Trey, what am I supposed to do?" Walter asked, knowing Trey was expecting more than he felt he could provide.

"Don't ask me. You're the lawyer. That's what I pay you for. You have a briefcase full of money. Make a miracle happen."

"Okay, but I need something to work with."

"How about this? Sgt. Turner threatened and attacked me during lockup last night," Trey added as he continued to fill him in on his little run-in with Sgt. Turner.

Thinking over Trey's comments, Ashcroft came up with an idea. He signaled for Sgt. Turner and Lt. Dawson to return. Ashcroft received a phone text as Sgt. Turner and Lt. Dawson entered the room.

"All right, we're ready to proceed. Maybe I misunderstood the bailiff's response. What charges are you holding my client on?"

"There is no misunderstanding, Trey is being held for two counts of murder and suspicion of eight counts of murder," Sgt. Turner answered.

"This is ridiculous. Next, you'll be saying my client's a serial killer."

"We have a witness who is willing to testify they saw Mr. Wilkens kill both men. We also have reason to believe that Mr. Wilkens was responsible for the murders of his rival, Donta Wilson, and four of his men as well as three smalltime drug dealers found dead in the projects earlier this morning," Lt. Dawson added. "Five of these men were known associates of yours. What I don't understand is, why would you kill them?" Sgt. Turner asked.

"Exactly, why would my client kill these men if, as you claim, they were his friends?"

"The question was directed to your client."

"My client has been advised not to answer any more questions. It is clear that outside of this eye witness for the two counts of murder, you have no physical evidence to tie my client to the other eight murders. So at this point, legally you can only pursue the two counts of murder. Oh before I forget, I would like to make a formal complaint on behalf of my client."

"Regarding?" Sgt. Turner asked.

"Two nights ago, my client was approached by an individual at his club. The individual demanded my client to help him acquire drugs and pay him $5000. If my client refused to give in to his demands, he threatened to go to the police and state that my client made a threat against his life."

"Ashcroft, how is this relevant to this case?"

"I'm not sure if it is, but considering you guys are all about justice, we decided you needed to know the person that is blackmailing my client is Perry Taylor. I wouldn't be a bit surprised if this so call eye witness is Perry."

Both Lt. Dawson and Sgt. Turner were left speechless from Ashcroft's accusation.

"Okay, well after we get done here, I will send Officer O'Neil in to take your client's official statement and have someone pick Mr. Taylor up for questioning," Lt. Dawson responded.

"I'm sure my client would appreciate that."

"I bet he would," Sgt. Turner added.

"Sgt. Turner, this entire case is beginning to appear like a frame job. It appears as if every dead body that turns up, you attempt to pin on my client."

"That's insane," Sgt. Turner responded.

"Lt. Dawson, I'm aware that you transferred to this precinct from L.A. five months ago."

Both Sgt. Turner and Lt. Dawson were surprised that Ashcroft had background information on Lt. Dawson.

"What does my background have to do with this case?"

"I only mentioned this to establish how new you are to this situation."

"What situation?" Both men asked.

"I was wondering if you're aware of the years of harassment my client has received from Sgt. Turner?"

"Harassment? Now you're really reaching," Sgt. Turner responded, laughing. "This is a serious matter. Lt. Dawson, I have reason to believe that these bogus charges of two counts of murder and the suspicion in the other eight counts of murders are nothing more than a conspiracy orchestrated by Sgt. Turner to frame my client due to the hatred he has for him. Sgt. Turner has had a vendetta against my client ever since his son was killed outside my client's club five years ago."

Sgt. Turner was outraged that Trey and his sleazy lawyer would use his son's death as an angle. "This is total bullshit! Don't you dare bring my son into this!"

"Ashcroft, these are legitimate charges. We have ten dead bodies in the county morgue as we speak," Lt. Dawson replied.

"I'm not disputing the body count. I'm wondering why is it that every crime Sgt. Turner investigates, my client always becomes his main suspect."

"Because your client is the one committing the crimes."

"Sgt. Turner, isn't it true that you've had twelve unsuccessful attempts to frame my client with charges from racketeering to murder within the past six years?"

"I'm an officer of the law. We as law enforcement officers don't attempt to frame anybody. Those charges were all legitimate. Besides, that was then. How about we stick with the here and now?"

"All right, if you insist. Isn't it true that while securing my client to a holding cell last night, you told him and I quote, '*I got your ass this time,*' and '*I will kill you,*' before attacking him?"

Richard noticed the surprising expression on William's face. "You're taking what I said out of context. He threatened my family. Look, for years Trey has managed to con and buy his way out of every crime he has committed. I was simply implying that this time, all the money in the world isn't going to help him."

"I'm sure that's what you meant Sgt. Turner. It's officers like you that give policemen a bad reputation," Ashcroft replied sarcastically.

"Wait a minute..."

"No, you wait a minute. On behalf of my client, I'm filing charges of harassment against Sgt. Richard Turner. Under the condition of personal interest, I'm also requesting that Sgt. Turner be barred from the pre-trial hearing."

Sgt. Turner was livid. He had dealt with Ashcroft on several occasions and knew that he was an outstanding lawyer. However, he never saw this one coming.

"You slimy bastard, personal interest my ass! I'm going to nail your client's ass to the wall. He's a murdering drug-trafficking dope peddler. The truth, is he's at the end of his rope, trying to find some loop hole to save his sorry ass. Ashcroft, you know he killed all ten of those men, and he's going to pay for it."

"Sgt. Turner, those are accusations that have to be proven. Even if that was so, my client is innocent until proven guilty in a court of law, by a judge or jury of his peers if he so chooses. Its call due process. That's not something that you have the right to decide. See, that's exactly what I'm talking about. Your hatred for my client has blinded your judgment as an officer of the law. You are emotionally involved due to the loss of your son. I do not feel that you are capable of presenting a judge with a fair judgment in this case without making it personal."

It was apparent that Ashcroft's idea was working. Sgt. Turner had lost his cool while Lt. Dawson was amazed at what he was hearing. "Save the crap, Ashcroft. Your client is a relentless killer, and you know it."

Trey sat, silently pleased as his lawyer and Sgt. Turner continued to go at each other.

Lt. Dawson listened to both men argue as he thought about how bad it would look to the judge at the pretrial. He knew Ashcroft was not going to back down.

"Ashcroft give us a moment. Richard, come with me."

Sgt. Turner walked away from the table and followed Lt. Dawson out of the room with a puzzled look on his face.

"Richard, I don't like this any more than you but, under the circumstances, I'm going to have to pull you from the pretrial hearing."

Sgt. Turner was stunned. He could not believe Lt. Dawson's decision to remove him from the pretrial. He felt betrayed by his own superior.

"William, don't do this. This is exactly what he wants. I'm the arresting officer. I should be there."

"Richard, what other choice do I have? They have us by the balls. He's within his rights. Besides, he has a strong argument for harassment against you. If we don't do this, it could hurt our case further. You and Trey definitely have history. Not to mention the fact that if Trey can produce an eye witness that can place Perry in his club two days ago, his creditability is shot, and we basically have no case against him. Don't worry, I'm going to stand in for you at the pre-trial."

"Fine, I'll go along with it. You know that whole blackmail complaint was too convenient."

"I agree, but considering the fact that Trey has not seen our witness makes their argument very strong."

Trey and Ashcroft continued to talk strategy as they waited for Lt. Dawson and Sgt. Turner to return.

"It looks like they're starting to panic. Do you think Lt. Dawson bought into my harassment claim?"

"I'm not sure, but I think we're about to find out," Ashcroft responded quietly as the door opened.

"Okay, as you requested, Sgt. Turner has been removed from the pretrial hearing. I will attend the hearing in his place."

"Okay, sound like we're in agreement!" Ashcroft answered with a big smirk on his face.

*   *   *   *   *

Half an hour later, Ashcroft was sitting in the left front row of the courtroom as he waited for his client to enter. Trey entered the courtroom escorted by the bailiff. Prosecuting Attorney Nina Johnson entered the courtroom with her briefcase in hand. Lt. Dawson walked in as well and took a seat in the front row to the right. Everyone stood as the Judge entered and then swiftly took his seat. "Everyone, please be seated."

"First case, State vs. Trey Wilkens!" The Circuit Clerk called out.

"Mr. Wilkens, we meet again. Who is representing Mr. Wilkens?" Judge Walsh asked.

"Your Honor, I'm representing Mr. Wilkens."

"I had to ask. You guys are becoming regulars in my court room. I see here that we have Mr. Wilkens for two counts of murder. Mr. Wilkens, I'm getting tired of seeing you in my court room."

Nina, a forty-one year old, short, petite blonde with smoker's teeth, wanted to put the pressure on Ashcroft and Trey. The newly elected mayor turned up the heat on Nina when he heard about all of the murders in his city over the last twenty-four hours. He was demanding results. Pushing this to go to trial and getting a guilty conviction against Trey would be a terrific accomplishment in his first term.

"Your Honor, the state is seeking to charge Mr. Wilkens with two counts of murder."

"Mr. Ashcroft, how does your client plead?"

"My client pleads not guilty."

"Ms. Johnson, do you have anything to add?"

"Yes, Your Honor. The state feels that due to the severity of the defendant's crimes, we request that he be denied bail."

"Your Honor, with all due respect to the state. My client has no prior convictions. He's a family man and a respected business man in the community."

The hostility between the two of them was obvious to everyone in the court room. They had gone head to head over a dozen times, all ending with Ashcroft victorious. Nina was determined not to let this opportunity slip away.

"Your Honor, this is serious. The defendant is running around town killing people with no regard to human life or the law. He is a vigilante who has had numerous run-ins with the law. His arrest record speaks for itself. Mr. Wilkens is a threat to society and a risk to flight. Therefore, we are requesting that no bail be granted."

Ashcroft knew Nina was out for revenge. He glanced down at her curvy hips, remembering back last year when he fucked her in one of the courtroom bathroom stalls. Although he loved her spontaneous sexual desires, he was only using her. They dated for three years and kept their relationship hidden from the public. She finally broke it off when she learned he was engaged to be married last September.

"Your Honor, that is about as ridiculous as the charges being brought against my client."

Nina wasted no time slicing into Ashcroft's comments. "Tell that to the family members of those two men. Your Honor, how can we be sure Mr. Wilkens will not harm anyone else?"

"You can't ask for assurance against a verdict that has yet to be determined."

Judge Walsh banged his gavel after getting tired of hearing both attorneys argue back and forth. "Enough! This is a court of law, not a national debate. Mr. Ashcroft, would your client like to speak on his own behalf before I make my ruling?" Trey whispered into Ashcroft's ear reminding him about the harassment card. "Your Honor, my client would like to file a grievance against Sgt. Turner for conspiring to frame him for ten counts of murder."

"What basis of support do you have for this accusation?" Judge Walsh asked, not believing a word of Trey's complaint although he knew he had to entertain it.

"Sgt. Turner is trying to destroy my client's life as part of a personal vendetta he has because of the unfortunate death of his son which took place outside my client's club five years ago. Sgt. Turner has arrested my client over a dozen times in the last five years. His charges ranging from racketeering to murder but have never convicted my client of any of these crimes."

Nina laughed in disbelief at Ashcroft's remarks. "That's absurd!"

"Is it? Last night during lock-up, Sgt. Turner threatened and assaulted my client. Other inmates witnessed the incident."

Judge Walsh remembered the case against Trey for the murder of Sgt. Turner's son. He presided over the case. Judge Walsh recalled how angry Sgt. Turner was with the verdict.

"Is Sgt. Turner present?"

"No, Your Honor. At the plaintiff's request, Sgt. Turner was removed from this case due to allegations of conflict of interest. I will be handling Mr. Wilkens investigation," Lt. Dawson said, standing up to address the judge.

"Very well, Mr. Wilkens please stand."

Trey stood and faced the Judge as he waited for him to give his decision. His facial expression was firm. No sign of nervousness. Trey was as cool as a hooker on a date.

"Mr. Wilkens, fortunately, I am familiar with your previous proceedings. I handled several of those cases personally. Now, if you feel you have been mistreated or falsely accused of any crime by the city's law enforcement, I urge you to file a grievance. However, today's preliminary trial is to determine whether or not you will be granted bail. During this period the state will also explore its options to determine whether we have enough evidence to move forward with an indictment against you. Do you understand these rights Mr. Wilkens?"

"Yes, Your Honor."

"Going against my better judgment, I will grant bail at the sum of two hundred thousand dollars. Mr. Wilkens, don't make me regret giving you this bail. I will further review this case in my chambers and make a ruling whether the State of Illinois should proceed with an indictment against you, Mr. Wilkens."

Trey was relieved to hear that he would be granted bail.

"Thank you."

Once Judge Walsh banged his gavel, Trey knew he had dodged the first bullet. He turned and noticed Nina staring at him with a disgusted expression. She was furious that Ashcroft had convinced the judge that Trey was not a flight risk. Trey's smirk only made her more determined to seek conviction against him. Nina approached both Trey and Walter. Trey unfastened Ashcroft's briefcase. He opened it to show Nina his bail money.

"I think I have enough money to make bail."

"You may have won this round, but trust me Mr. Wilkens, I will get this case to the Grand Jury. You better pray it doesn't make it to trial because the state will be seeking the death penalty."

"You are such a sore loser. I thought you'd be used to this by now," Ashcroft replied.

"Damn! That was cold. Maybe if you let him hit that again, he might let you finally win a case," Trey added sarcastically.

Embarrassed and speechless, Nina stormed out of the courtroom.

"I'll be right back. I've gotta post your bail."

"Walter, you did pretty good today."

As Ashcroft left the courtroom, Trey noticed Lt. Dawson standing in the back of the courtroom. He gave Trey a menacing stare before exiting.

CHAPTER 9

UNFORGIVEN TRAGEDY

Later that evening at Candi's suite, Candi and Trey were cuddled up under the sheets having sex. Candi was sitting on top of Trey humping up and down as his hands were gripping her voluptuous ass while continuously meeting her in midstride.

"Oh, Trey fuck me baby, it's yours."

Trey suddenly swung her around, switching positions. He began roughly pushing up and down on her after spreading her legs further apart. She felt pain and pleasure all at the same time as he continued to penetrate her. She wrapped her legs around his, thinking how complete she felt.

Candi sunk her nails deep into the skin of Trey's upper back. Moaning, she continued clawing him as she began to have an orgasm.

"Trey... I'm coming!"

Trey stuck his tongue in her mouth, and then began to passionately kiss her neck as she continued to moan. He humped faster and then groaned as he climaxed. He then rolled over and grabbed the glass of water off the night stand. Practically out of breath, he swallowed the entire glass down. Candi lays her head down on Trey's shoulder in thought after having the most intense half hour of sex in years.

"Trey, can I ask you something?"

"Ask," he replied as he placed the glass back on the night stand.

"How did you and Monica meet?"

"Why do you want to know?"

"Well, with everything you said, she doesn't sound like your type," Candi said as she rubbed his chest, admiring his chiseled pecs.

"And what's my type?"

"You know, sexy but a little ghetto. Kind of down for whatever."

"You mean like you?"

"No, that's not what I meant."

"Yeah, well Monica is different. That's one of the things that attracted me to her."

"How did you meet her anyway?"

Trey thought back to the day he first met Monica. "We met at St. Louis Lambert Airport. Monica was relocating from St. Louis to Chicago. It was her first airplane flight, and she was nervous. Her seat was in the same row as mine. We talked the entire flight and exchanged numbers."

"How did she react when she found out what you do for a living?"

"She threatened to leave me."

"But she didn't. Why?"

"By the time she found out, her feelings were too deep."

"So you were her first?"

"Yep."

Candi gave a phony smile after hearing Trey admit to taking Monica's virginity. Not knowing how to respond, she said the first thing that came to mind.

"So you got the church girl all dirty."

"Monica's a good woman."

Candi rolled over and climbed on top of Trey.

"Trey, I know you care for her, but she's all wrong for you. She can never please you the way I can."

Candi raised back the covers and slid downward. She touched his penis and started to masturbate him. Candi licked his penis as if it were a lollipop before motioning for him to place it in her mouth. Trey stopped Candi, pushing her away.

"What's wrong? Where are you going?"

"I have something to take care of," Trey responded after climbing out of the bed. He grabbed his clothes and headed to the bathroom.

*   *   *   *   *

Trey returned from the bathroom after showering, fully dressed.

"Trey, don't leave, let's talk about this. You know we're good together."

"Candi, we are good together. I just think this may be bad timing," Trey responded as he slid on his jacket and headed for the door.

"Do you think we have a chance of getting back what we once had?"

"Honestly, I don't know."

"Are you coming back?"

"Yes, I'll call you later," Trey replied before leaving.

*   *   *   *   *

Sgt. Turner was sitting at a table in the middle of Fabatini's Italian Restaurant having dinner with his wife and talking about Trey's case.

"Are you serious? You're off the case?" she asked.

"It sure looks that way. Trey filed a complaint against me today accusing me of framing him for murder."

"Is there any truth to it?"

"Ruth, you know me better than that. As much as I would love to put a bullet in him for killing our son, I have to leave his fate in the hands of God."

Ruth spotted Lt. Dawson approaching. "Good evening, William."

"Hello Ruth. It's good to see you again."

"William, what are you doing here?" Sgt. Turner asked.

"Picking up some takeout for me and the Misses."

"How is Mary Ann doing?" Ruth pleasantly asked.

"She's great. I tell you, this pregnancy has turned her into a health freak. She refuses to eat anything besides salads."

"It's natural. This is her first pregnancy. She just wants to make sure nothing goes wrong."

The restaurant host approached. "Lt. Dawson, your food is ready."

"Okay, thank you. William, tell Mary Ann if she needs anything, don't hesitate to call."

"I will do that, Ruth. Do you mind if I borrow your husband for a second?"

"No, not at all," she answered as she added more pepper to her mashed potatoes.

The two men walked over to the bar area.

"What's up William?"

"I guess you heard about Trey making bail?"

"I heard. Two hundred thousand dollars, that's petty cash to him. It's like no matter what he does, him and his scumbag lawyer always find a loop hole to work the system."

"The indictment was rejected by Judge Walsh. Three witnesses came forward to corroborate his story. It looks like we are back to square one. We need the murder weapon. The bullets didn't match the gun retrieved from his club."

"I read the report. He had a permit for the gun. Trey knows how to cover his tracks. Richard, I hate to be the one giving you this news…"

"What's going on?"

William placed his hand on Richard's shoulder, hoping to soften the blow he was about to deliver. "As your friend and superior officer, I suggest that you get yourself a good attorney. Trey and his attorney have just brought the fight to us."

"It almost sounds as if I'm the one on trial. What am I missing?"

"Richard, Internal Affairs is looking into Trey's allegations of you framing him."

"Since when did the word of a drug lord become superior to the word of a highly decorated law enforcement officer?"

Reluctantly, William decided to tell him what evidence they had. "Apparently, two inmates from lockup came forward and supported Trey's claim. They stated that last night they witnessed you threaten and attack him." Seemingly frustrated, Richard thought about his actions from the night before. He knew he had crossed the line despite being provoked.

 "That piece of shit! He's doing what he does best. Manipulating the system."

"Richard, I have to ask. Did you do what he's claiming you did?"

Richard knew that William did not have to share the information he did. However, he wasn't sure if he was asking as his friend or an officer of the law supporting Internal Affairs.

"Last night, Trey threatened to harm my daughter. William, I'm not going to let him take another child away from me. I will die before I allow that to happen."

William remembered reading the article of his son getting gunned down at Trey's club.

"I understand. Hey, what's the story on the two inmates? Do they have issues with you as well?"

"Those punks would sell their own mother down the river for a fast buck. Look, if they want to suspend me for doing my job then they can take this badge and shove it."

Sensing Richard was having a hard time dealing with the pressure Trey and his attorney were applying on him, William figured he would try to assure him that he was in his corner.

"Don't quit on me. I need you. You are the only one that knows Trey well enough to bring him down. Besides, don't do what he wants you to do."

Realizing William was probably right, he decided not to give up.

"Thanks, that means a lot to know I can count on you. I'll do what I can to help. Do me a favor though. Be careful. The one thing I've learned about him over the years is to never underestimate him."

Richard and William shook hands and parted ways. Richard rejoined his wife. He sat at the table staring at his food speechless.

"Honey, is everything okay?"

"No! Everything is not okay. Our son was murdered by this wannabe, larger than life, drug lord who's running around town killing people as if life comes a dime a dozen. Meanwhile, yours truly, the good guy, gets investigated by Internal Affairs for what? Doing his fuckin' job! Isn't our justice system wonderful?"

"Richard, please calm down. You're making a scene," Ruth said, stunned by Richard's comments.

Richard cut off a small portion of steak and stared at the medium rare cooked meat. "You're right. Lets' go. I've lost my appetite anyway. Waiter! Bring me my check!"

*   *   *   *   *

At an undisclosed safe house, Perry was placed under protective custody. He was sitting at the living room table playing poker with the two detectives. "Read them and weep, Queen Elizabeth and her two sisters."

As he laid down his cards, several men charged through the door with Uzis and began shooting. Both detectives reached for their guns but were shot in the process. Terrified, Perry crawled under the table, hoping to keep from getting shot.

"Come here, bitch!" Half-Dead said to Perry as he grabbed him by his shirt collar.

He slapped him twice before delivering a gut wrenching punch to his stomach. Smiling, Half-Dead shoved Perry toward Crazy Willie.

"Man tie his punk-ass up!"

Half-Dead, a short, stocky dark skinned lunatic and former eastside killer for hire, thrived on killing. His sick twisted mind should have a strait jacket strapped to it. There was no limit to what he would or wouldn't do. His running buddy, Crazy Willie, a short, chubby thug with braids, was recently released from prison after serving a five-year stint. His heavy frame and long thick beard gave him an intimidating appearance. He also smelled like he hadn't bathed in weeks. Crazy

Willie began tying Perry to one of the living room chairs as Trey walked in.

"Trey, please don't kill me. I didn't want to say nothing. They forced me to talk." Trey approached Perry holding a Black & Mild cigar in his left hand. Half-Dead returned with a gasoline can. He began splashing gas on the walls, furniture and carpet before pouring gasoline on Perry.

"You made a big mistake Perry. I play for keeps. Nobody snitches on me and get away with it."

Perry continued to plead for his life as tears flowed down his face.

"Trey, I didn't want no part of this. Please, I promise to keep my mouth shut. Just don't kill me."

"You already had that opportunity, and you fucked up! You were just in the wrong place at the wrong time. Maybe in your next life, you'll remember never to cross me."

Trey took one last puff from his cigar before dropping it into the gasoline on the floor. The cigar ignited the fire and within seconds, Perry was covered in flames. Unable to free himself from the chair, Perry yelled as he burned to death.

*   *   *   *   *

Monica stepped out of the shower. She wrapped a bath towel around her body and used a hand towel to dry off her hair. She walked out of the bathroom and into the bedroom when she heard the phone ring.

"Hello."

"Hi Monica, its Meechi. Have you heard from Trey?"

"No. I haven't seen him since he left the family reunion yesterday. It seems like he doesn't take his marriage seriously enough to call or come home."

"He must still be in jail," Meechi replied.

Monica was almost afraid to ask. "In jail! Why is he in jail?"

"I'm not really sure. Last night the cops arrested him for murdering two of our employees."

"Meechi, that doesn't make any sense. Why would Trey kill his own employees?"

"Good question. Did he say anything to you yesterday?"

Monica recalled the shooting yesterday and wondered if that had anything to do with it. "Not really, but I was afraid that something like this would happen. Yesterday Trey left the family reunion in rage because a couple of guys tried to kill him at his mother's house. Are these the same guys he killed?"

Meechi figured he'd lay his ground work attempting to convince Monica that Trey was losing his edge.

"No, I think those guys were from Donta's crew. Trey killed Donta earlier before coming to the family reunion."

Monica was speechless. She did not know what to say. Not to mention, she was wondering why Meechi was sharing this with her.

"Did he tell you this himself?"

"He didn't have to, I was there," Meechi answered.

"When Trey came to the club last night, he didn't mention anything about someone trying to kill him."

Monica now seriously sensed something was not right with Meechi and Trey's relationship, but she wasn't going to let on that she was suspicious.

"When was the last time you talked to Trey?"

"Last night. He called me from the police station. I contacted his lawyer and took him some money for bail."

"I hope everything is okay."

"You know Monica, Trey and I go way back. I'll always have his back, but I have to say this to you. Lately, Trey hasn't been himself. He has been stirring up trouble with the other rival cliques and making bad business decisions. He's got too much on his plate. If you ask me, his priority should be at home with you and his son."

As odd as it sounded coming from Meechi, she knew he had a valid point.

"I couldn't agree more," she responded.

"Look, don't say anything to him about our conversation because he's been really edgy. The last thing this organization needs is trouble at the ranks."

"Okay. Meechi, if you hear from Trey please tell him to call me."

"For you anything. By the way, how's little Trey doing?" With a dirty grin on his face Meechi thought he'd stick the knife in the wound and turn it.

"He's fine."

"Monica, for all that it's worth, I think you are a very special lady."

"Thank you Meechi. Well, I have..."

"I mean it. Trey doesn't deserve you. He doesn't treat you with the respect you deserve. If you were my wife, I would be home making love to you every night," Meechi said after cutting her off as she tried to end the call.

Monica paused for a second before speaking. She was convinced that Meechi had an agenda. If Trey knew that Meechi was hitting on her, he'd kill him with no hesitation.

"I'm sure the woman you marry will appreciate that dedication."

"Listen, I have to go. I'll talk to you later. Stay sweet," Meechi said before ending the call.

Hanging up the phone, Monica walked over to the mirror. Staring at her own reflection, she thought about the weird conversation she had just endured. *What was that all about?*

* * * * *

Sgt. Turner and his wife climbed into his four-door, Silver 2014 Dodge Charger and buckled their seat belts.

"Honey, I'm sorry about earlier. All the stress from this case is getting to me." Ruth leaned over and kissed him on the cheek. "I know. Try not to worry so much. William will take care of everything. We can't control what is not within our reach."

"So true," Richard replied, smiling as he turned west bound out of the restaurant parking lot.

Two men were sitting in a four-door, black 1997 SS Impala, Limited Edition with all tinted windows. The vehicle started trailing them. As they stopped at the red light, the black Impala pulled in front of their car. Two men jumped out of the passenger side doors with Uzis, shooting at the couple's vehicle.

"Sweetheart, get down!" Richard immediately shoved Ruth's head down into the car seats as he ducked for safety as well. He grabbed his CB radio and called in for help.

"This is Unit One to base. Come in."

"Unit One, this is base, over," the Dispatcher answered.

"I need some back up, I'm under heavy fire."

"Unit One, what's your location?"

"I'm at Route 19 and Kostner Avenue."

"Unit One, units are on their way."

"Why are they shooting at us?" Ruth screamed, horrified as the front windshield shattered.

"I don't think this is a good time to ask them."

Richard knew if he didn't make a move soon, they would both be dead. He unbuckled his holster and pulled his gun. Slowly, he opened the car door.

Ruth grabbed his arm in concern realizing her husband might be committing suicide by stepping in the line of gun fire.

"Richard, please be careful."

The two shooters heard the sirens from the responding units and decided to retreat. "Let's get out of here," Shooter One suggested to Shooter Two. They stopped firing and started easing toward the SS Impala.

Richard jumped out and fired several shots at the shooters. He hit Shooter Two in the right shoulder. He used the open door of his vehicle for cover as both men fired back before jumping into the car and speeding off. As the SS Impala drove away, Richard got a look at the license plate. *T E W 1 7 5 4* he thought to himself as he tried to memorize it. He walked back to the car to check on Ruth. Richard noticed her slumped down on the seat bleeding from a bullet wound on the left portion of her chest. Richard frantically grabbed the radio.

"I need an ambulance! My wife has been shot."

CHAPTER 10

OUT OF REACH

It was 2:15 am, several hours later at Memorial Hospital. Lt. Dawson entered the emergency entrance and spotted Sgt. Turner pacing back and forth.

"How is she?"

He stopped pacing momentarily. "I don't know. She lost a lot of blood. William, if she does not make it my life is over."

"Don't talk like that. She will pull through this. Ruth's a fighter." William said, taking a seat in one of the empty chairs.

"What about the shooters? Did you catch them?"

"Unfortunately no, the Impala was reported stolen."

"That's just great!"

Dr. Bradley approached the two men. "Excuse me, Sgt. Turner?"

"Doc, I hope you have some good news."

"I'm sorry. Your wife did not make it. We tried everything humanly possible."

"Thank you, Doc. I know you and your staff did everything you could to save her."

Sgt. Turner shook Dr. Bradley's hand and then watched silently as he walked away.

He wanted to cry but didn't have the energy. Totally devastated, Richard took a seat in one of the chairs. He played the shooting back in his mind. "Richard, I'm sorry."

"Ruth was my rock. She meant everything to me. First I lost my son, now my wife."

Sgt. Turner walked away from Lt. Dawson heading toward Ruth's room. He opened the door and saw her body covered by a white sheet. Her hand dangled over the bed rail. Crying as he walked up to her, Richard touched her hand and held it. He stared at the engraved bracelet around her wrist as he stood over her body. He had just giving her the bracelet for her birthday. Closing his eyes, Sgt. Turner thought back to the day they were married. He removed the sheet from over her head.

"Sweetheart, I'm so sorry. You didn't deserve this. This should have been me. I promise you, if it's the last thing I do, I'll make Trey pay for this."

As Sgt. Turner left the room, Lt. Dawson walked up to him.

"William, I'm done! This time, Trey has pushed me too far. Internal Affairs wants my badge, well here it is."

In frustration Sgt. Turner removed his badge and handed it to William.

"Don't do this, Richard."

"My wife lost her life tonight because some self-righteous son of a bitch tried to kill me. Now, it's his turn to die." Sgt. Turner walked away, heading toward the exit.

"You can't take the law into your own hands."

"Look, I know you're trying to help, but right now no one can."

"I won't let you do this, Richard."

"No one is going to stand in the way of me putting an end to this. Not you, Internal Affairs or anyone else," Sgt. Turner said before exiting the hospital.

*   *   *   *   *

Trey was sitting in his black reclining chair with his legs propped while his barber and manicurist worked on his hair and nails. Meechi, Red and Tony enters his office. "What's up, Trey?"

"How long have you been out?" Meechi ask curiously.

"A few hours."

"Shatina said you wanted to talk to us." Meechi and Red took a seat as Tony remained standing.

"That's right. As you guys are aware by now, somebody put a price on my head. What pisses me off about this is they had the balls to pay two of my own men to carry out the job."

The three of them had a dumbfounded look on their face as they didn't quite know what to expect. Tony's heart started pounding. He figured Trey called them there to kill them. Meechi tried to stay cool as Trey stared directly at him.

"You mean Terrell and Derek?"

"Yeah."

"Damn! That shit is foul. When we find the mutha-fucka responsible, I would personally like to put a bullet in his head," Meechi added.

Tracey walked into Trey's office, interrupting their meeting. "Trey, can I talk to you?" Tracey, one of Trey's handlers, asked, stumbling into his office smelling like liquor and weed. Tracey was a tall, skinny man with long permed hair.

"Fool, can't you see we're busy?" Red shouted.

"What do you want, Tracey?" Meechi asked.

"Trey, I didn't mean to interrupt. I saw your car parked out front and decided to stop by to drop off this month's take."

Tracey saw Meechi and Red's car out front as well. He was hoping that Trey wouldn't have time to talk to him so he wouldn't have to explain why his money was short.

"Not now, just give Meechi the money and leave," Trey replied.

Standing to the right of Meechi, Tracey pulled out the wad of money and handed it to him and turned to leave.

"Let's see what we got. Thirty-two, thirty-three... Hold on Tracey, There's supposed to be four grand not thirty-four hundred. Why are you short again?"

Tracey glanced at Trey. He knew he'd better do some fast talking.

"Tracey, where is the rest of my money?"

"I'm running a little short. Give me two days, and I promise I'll have it. Five-O has been all over my set. Last night I lost a quarter-ounce trying to ditch 'em."

"Let me make sure I heard you correctly. You lost a quarter-ounce of cocaine, and you're telling me that you are a little short. Six hundred dollars is more than a little short." Trey wasn't buying Tracey's excuse.

"Just give me a little more time. I swear I will have your money."

Trey noticed Tracey's glassy eyes and dry lips. He began to understand why Tracey was constantly short.

"How much more time do you need?"

"A couple days."

"How about a week," Trey asked being sarcastic.

"Sure, that's cool."

Tracey glanced around the room and noticed Red and Meechi laughing as Tony stood next to Meechi in silence with a serious expression on his face.

"Every week it seems like you're getting worse and worse, which makes me wonder, are you smoking my shit?"

Afraid of what he hoped wouldn't happen, Tracey began stuttering uncomfortably.

"Nah, Trey I ain't smoking. I've just been dealing with a few personal problems."

More convinced than ever that Tracey was smoking his work, Trey snapped. He stood up, shaking off the barber and manicurist.

"Stop! Both of you get out!"

The barber and manicurist both wasted no time packing up their stuff and hurrying out Trey's office. "Didn't I have a talk with you last week about this shit?"

"Yeah, I know I said..."

"You said you wouldn't let it happen again. Isn't that what you said?"

"I did but..."

"You also promised to have all my money. So lets' see, six hundred, plus four hundred, plus two hundred, is what Tracey?"

"Tw-tw-tw-elve hundred."

"That's right, twelve hundred dollars. I'm glad to see you can still count because you better have twelve hundred more dollars on you."

"Trey, please, give me a few more days. You know I'm good for it," Tracey begged, sensing Trey had bad intentions in mind. He slowly started easing towards the door.

"The only thing you're good for is smoking up my shit!

Trey approached Red and grabbed his nickel-plated three-eighty pistol from his back, turned and fired three shots into Tracey's chest. Tony jumped in shock as he watched Tracey hit the floor. Trey calmly walked back to his desk and sat on the edge of the desk with gun in hand. He faced the three of them and noticed the look of disbelief.

"What! Anybody got a problem with this?"

The three of them knew if they said yes, he'd probably shoot them as well.

"No. No problem at all," Meechi answered as Red and Tony nodded their heads in agreement.

"Then what the fuck are y'all waiting on? Get this dead muthafucka off my floor!"

Trey pulled out his handkerchief and wiped his prints off the gun before handing it back to Red.

Red and Tony picked up Tracey's body and carried him out of Trey's office.

Tony opened the back entrance door as the two of them struggled to carry Tracey's body out to Red's truck. Meechi walks up to Red and Tony.

"Dump the body in Molly's Creek. Make sure you strip him clean."

"Did you see that shit? We all knew Tracey was smoking but damn, I didn't see that one coming. It was as if he was sending us a message. Then the look he gave us afterwards," Red said, thinking about how cold Trey eyes were when he shot Tracey.

"I'm not surprised. However, I was thinking that could have been one of us," Tony said, starting to panic as he remembered Trey telling him the next time it would be him and his family.

Meechi felt his leverage slipping. He touched Red on the shoulder trying to reassure his confidence. "Trust me. This will all be over tonight. Out with the old and in with the new. Just get rid of the body and hurry back."

Meechi walked away, heading back inside the club. The two men continued to struggle as they loaded Tracey into the truck.

"Man, for a dead person you got some funky ass breathe," Red said to the corpse as Tony closed the trunk door.

"Did you see his expression when he said someone paid Terrell and Derek to kill him?"

Both men climbed into the truck. "Yeah, it was as if he knew it was us."

* * * * *

Trey turned on the lights and walked over to the pool table. He pulled out four quarters and slid them into the coin slot. Meechi entered the room and joined Trey. "Would you like a little competition?" Meechi asked, pulling out a roll of money and placing it on the rail of the pool table.

"I see you're feeling a little lucky," Trey responded.

"I've got five hundred dollars that say I don't need luck to win."

Trey pulled out his money clip with nothing but hundreds. He opened the gold money clip and laid five crisp one hundred dollar bills on the table.

"Okay, if you insist. What's your game?"

"Nine Ball," Meechi answered as he walked over to the pool cue rack.

Trey racked the balls accordingly. He grabbed the cue ball and walked over to the head of the table. Meechi handed him a pool cue as they prepared to flip for the break.

"Call it in the air," Meechi said as he tossed a quarter in the air.

"Tails," Trey replied as they both watched the coin drop on the slate.

Once the coin landed on heads, Trey handed him the cue ball. Meechi chalked-up his cue and prepared to break.

Confident that he could break and run out, Meechi started to brag. "Looks like the flip was in my favor. That's the nature of the game. You can win or lose any given day."

Trey stood off to the left of the pool table, waiting for Meechi to break the pool balls. "Remember, don't scratch on the break."

Meechi had never beaten Trey in Nine Ball. As good as he was, he would always come up short. Trey's comment added more pressure as he was hoping for the perfect break.

The cue ball smashed into the nine balls. The Two Ball and Six Ball were pocketed on the break. Meechi smiled as he chalked up his cue.

"One Ball, left corner pocket." He pocketed the One Ball. Meechi re-chalked his cue. "Three Ball, side pocket." The Three Ball bounced into the pocket. Walking around the table, Meechi grabbed the chalk and chalked up as he studied his next shot.

Trey remained poised as he waited for his opening. "Four Ball, left corner pocket." The ball, seemingly on its way down in the pocket, bounced out. Meechi stepped away upset. Trey chalked up his cue as he studied the shot before approaching it. Meechi looked on, hoping he would miss. Trey stepped into position to shoot the ball.

"Four Ball, left corner pocket."

After hitting the shot, his cue ball bounced two rails down toward the foot of the table, positioning him for a combination shot. "Five Ball will combo off the Nine Ball, pocketing the Nine Ball."

Trey chalked up and popped the shot into the pocket. "I'm surprised, you of all people should know that when you go up against me, you'll lose."

Meechi knew if he hadn't missed the Four Ball, he could have beat Trey.

Okay, Nine Ball is your game. Let's play double or nothing in Pocket Eight Ball."

"Rack' em."

Meechi fed the table four quarters in the coin slot and racked the balls.

Trey chalked up and broke the balls. He pocketed three balls, one solid and two stripes.

"I'll take stripes." Trey liked the setup for the striped balls.

"Listen Trey, we never got around to talking about the shooting."

Trey pocketed the first ball in. "It ain't much to it. Some snake ass bitch paid them to take me out. They missed, but I didn't," Trey said as he easily hit in another ball.

"Did they tell you who paid them to kill you?"

Trey hit in another ball before answering Meechi's question. "When someone tries to kill me, I don't put too much emphasis on talking."

Trey pocketed the Ten Ball. Meechi noticed Trey only had the Twelve and Eight Ball left. Trey hit a soft stroke pocketing the Twelve Ball.

"The other day at the club we didn't mean no disrespect by sitting at your table."

"Forget about it. All I want is the muthafucka who put Derek and Terrell up to killing me."

Trey chalked up his cue as he got set to pocket the Eight Ball in the right side pocket.

"I did some checking. It seems Shante has been bragging around town about being the one who put the price on your head."

"I guess he wants to be buried with his brother," Trey responded, pretending to buy into Meechi' s ploy.

Trey stared down the Eight Ball and paused as he prepared to hit the cue across table to pocket it.

"Do you want me to take care of him?" Meechi asked.

"No, leave him be for now. Business before pleasure. Tonight Big T will be here to close the deal. After we secure this deal with Big T, bring Shante' to me. I'ma cut his balls off and shove 'em down his throat."

After making preparations for his stroke, Trey took the shot. "Eight Ball, right corner pocket."

Meechi stood to the side, realizing he just lost another five hundred dollars.

"Damn! How you gon' beat me at my own game?"

Trey laid the pool cue down on the table and picked up the money. "Because that's what I do. Lock up for me. I'll see you later."

Meechi watched as Trey left the club. *Tonight is the night and this time, I won't miss.*

CHAPTER 11

DRASTIC DECISIONS

As Trey pulled into his subdivision, Sgt. Turner cautiously tailed him. Trey parked and climbed out of his vehicle. He started toward the building entrance. Sgt. Turner pulled his gun after parking. He opened his car door and stepped out when another car pulled up. Rodney, Trey's neighbor, was exiting the building when he stopped to talk to Trey.

"Hey Trey, I'm on my way down to your club. I heard my man Kells is performing tonight."

Sgt. Turner pointed his gun at Trey, but unfortunately, the idled vehicle waiting for Rodney prevented him from getting a clean shot. He lowered his gun and climbed back into his car.

"He'll be there. My man Dilemma and The Realist will be performing as well."

"Word, thanks man."

Rodney started toward his cousin's car, and Trey walked away heading into his condo. Sgt. Turner sat in the car thinking about his wife lying on the hospital bed.

Trey, you will pay for this, he thought to himself as he drove off.

* * * * *

Trey entered the condo. He walked into the bedroom as Monica was hanging up the phone.

"Good, you're home. I've been trying to reach you since the family reunion. Where have you been?"

"Why?" Trey asked, nonchalantly while taking off his jacket and hanging it in the closet. He casually loosened his tie.

"What kind of stupid question is that? I'm your wife or have you forgotten? You do live here, Trey!"

"Look, I don't want to hear this shit. Every time I walk through that door, you're ready to argue. I'm tired, irritated, and hungry. This is not the time to get on my case."

"I'm not arguing with you, I'm just concerned. Why is it that you always shut me out? Will you for once just talk to me?"

Trey laid down on the bed next to her. He could see the concern in her eyes and knew he owed her an explanation. Deep inside, he wanted things to be different, but he didn't know where to start.

"You want to talk? Okay, let's talk." Trey sat up in the bed.

Monica was surprised that for once Trey was willing to open up to her. Even though she wanted this, she wasn't sure what to expect.

"Over the past two days, I've been shot at, arrested and even killed several people."

"You killed people?"

"That's what I said. But, that ain't the best part. I found out that Meechi has been plotting to take me out so he can take over."

Monica suspicions were on point. Hearing Trey admit to killing someone made her decide not to tell him about the phone call from Meechi. She knew it would send him over the edge.

"I thought you and Meechi were close?"

Trey paused for a second, feeling hurt and betrayed by someone he considered to be his brother. "So did I, but the truth of the matter is you warned me. I never would have expected Meechi to pull something like this. But you best believe, I will take care of him."

Monica knew it would be silly to try and talk him out of it, and to her surprise she didn't want to. Meechi crossed the line, and she knew it would either be him or Trey. Speechless, Monica stared at him not sure what to say.

"So how's that for conversation? Now if you don't mind, I need to take a shower. I have a meeting later tonight and I need to be well rested," Trey said as he walked into the bathroom, closing the door behind him.

Monica picked up the telephone and called her best friend Tracy.

Tracy was just returning home from jogging when she heard the phone ringing. Sweat was pouring down the side of her face as she wiped herself off with a towel. Tracy and Monica had been friends since grade school. Tracy moved to Chicago three months before Monica's wedding. She hated the fact that she encouraged her friend to marry Trey.

"Hello?" Tracy replied, picking up the phone.

"Hey girl, how's it going?"

"Tired, just ran two miles."

"Listen I need to talk. Can you stop by here?"

"Sure what time?"

"Around six o'clock."

"Okay. What's going on?"

Monica could hear Trey moving around in the bathroom. "I can't talk now. I'll see you later," Monica answered before hanging up.

Tracy hung up the telephone and began wiping the sweat off her long beautiful chocolate legs. She sat down on the bed and unlaced her Nike tennis shoes. Thinking about Monica, she started wondering what

Monica wanted to talk about. Tracy pulled down the black biker shorts and headed to the bathroom to jump in the shower. *I wonder what you've done this time, you bastard. I told her to leave his ass.*

*   *   *   *   *

Meechi was sitting at the bar sipping on his drink when Trey entered the club.

"You're early," Meechi commented as Trey joined him at the bar.

"Candi asked me to meet her here. Have you seen her?" Trey asked, taking a seat on one of the stools.

"Come to think of it, she was here earlier."

Fred overheard Trey's conversation with Meechi. He reached under the bar shelf and grabbed the white envelope.

"Boss, Candi ask me to give you this," Fred said, handing him the envelope.

Trey opened the envelope and began reading the letter. Fred the bartender placed a napkin and Trey's usual, Rum and Coke with a twist of lime on the rocks in front of him.

"Here you go, boss."

Dear Trey,

I love you with all my heart. I know you are confused, so I decided to make the decision for you. This is hard for me but it is for the best. I don't want to be the cause for your marriage failing. This is goodbye. Please give Monica the chance she deserves to make things better between the two of you.

Love Always,

Candi.

Trey picked up the drink and swallowed it down.

"Is everything okay?" Meechi asked as he sat next to Trey wondering what she wrote. "She's gone."

Meechi took a swallow from his glass. "It's probably for the best. Candi would've been a distraction. Besides, you have the finest woman in Chicago at home taking care of your son."

Fred placed a second drink in front of Trey. Staring at it for a second, Trey downed it. "You're absolutely right."

*   *   *   *   *

Monica heard the knock at the door. She opened the door, after glancing through the peephole.

"Is he gone?" Tracy asked as she stepped inside the condo.

"Yes. He left about a half-hour ago."

They both hugged. Monica was so happy to see her friend. They hadn't spent much time together over the past six months because Tracy had recently started medical school.

"Okay girlfriend, spill the beans. What did he do this time?"

"I don't know where to start. Yesterday at the family reunion, everything was going fine when we suddenly heard gun shots. I rushed to the front of the house and Trey was lying on his mother's lawn."

"So someone shot him?" Tracy asked as she took a seat on the recliner. She sensed this was about to get juicy.

"Yes, fortunately for him, he was wearing his bulletproof vest. He left upset and never came home until earlier today."

As Monica paused, Tracy seemed confused wondering where this was going.

"So what happened next?"

"Well, a couple of hours before Trey came home, Meechi called asking me if I heard from Trey. First off, it was awkward. Once I told him no, he started rambling on about how Trey had snapped and he didn't know what Trey would do next."

Tracy was dying to hear more as she suddenly remembered the call she had received earlier from Meechi as well.

"Meechi called me earlier asking me if I wanted to go out with him. When I said I don't date drug dealers, he just laughed and said that I would change my mind once he becomes the man."

"Girl, Trey told me he killed several people because they were trying to kill him."

The look on Tracy's face said it all. She was totally stunned he shared this with Monica.

"What made him tell you this?"

"I knew something was wrong so I pressed him to talk to me. He told me that Meechi was the one trying to have him killed."

"That snake-ass punk. That explains his comments. All these years he's been with Trey, and now greed has got the best of him," Tracy said as she was thinking about everything Trey had done for Meechi. "You know I'm no big fan of Trey, but even he don't deserve this."

"That's not all. When Meechi called here earlier, he started talking about if I was his woman he'd be home making love to me every night."

Tracy was blown away. She knew Trey was going to kill him for sure.

"I'm sure Trey hit the roof when you told him this?"

"I didn't tell him."

"What! Girl have you lost your mind? Why didn't you tell him?"

"Trey was already upset and hurt about finding out Meechi was behind the shooting at his mother's house. I couldn't dare tell him this."

Tracy thought for a second, deciding whether or not to tell her what she had heard.

"How do you feel about this whole thing?"

"Well, I somewhat feel sorry for Trey. He told me the story about his father and how he was killed. Tracy, it's like history repeating itself for him."

"Honey, you know that's the nature of the beast. No one is beyond being an enemy."

One of the things that Monica loved the most about Tracy was the fact that she kept it real. "I know. Look, I don't condone killing at any form, but Meechi deserves to be gunned down and left for dead."

"All of that came out the mouth of a democratic woman that is against the death penalty," Tracy responded as the two of them shared a brief laugh.

"I was on the fence about whether or not I should tell you this. Then I thought, if it was me, I would want to know. Meechi told me that Candi was in town. She stopped by the club yesterday. He said she's here because she wants Trey back."

Monica knew that Candi was the first person Trey truly cared about. Her beef wasn't with Candi even if she was back for that reason. She only wanted her husband to live up to his vows.

"Before you say anything, I know Meechi only told me this because he was hoping that I would tell you. Even if she is here, let's not assume that he's been with her."

"If she's here, trust me Trey has seen her," Monica replied as she was beginning to wonder if all the drama she was dealing with was worth it. "Honestly, I've been considering leaving Trey. I told him that if things didn't improve I would file for a divorce."

Happy but surprised that Monica finally stood up to Trey, Tracy was interested to hear Trey's response.

"Good for you. I bet he didn't take that one well."

"He actually told me if I wanted out to leave. I'm not sure what to do."

As badly as Tracy wanted her best friend to be rid of Trey, she knew it had to be her own decision. "Girl, I can give you my two cents, but you have to decide for yourself. Look, I know how much you love him, but there comes a time when enough is enough. I think the best thing for you and the baby is for you to move out and come stay with me for a while."

Monica knew Tracy was right, although she couldn't imagine turning her back on Trey right now. "I know, but I can't leave him like this. Do you think it's too late to save my marriage?" Monica asked Tracy the question she had been pondering for weeks.

"Not if he wants the same thing. Let him decide who is more important to him, you or the streets."

Monica was almost afraid to ask what Tracy had in mind. Tracy always seemed to be one step ahead of men when it came to mind games.

"Ever since I married him, it seems as if the streets has meant more to him," Monica added.

"Okay, then let's get to the core of the apple. Call him and ask him to come home. Tell him you need to talk to him, and it can't wait. If he agrees, make him choose to stay home with you. Do whatever you have to do to convince him that he needs to be here with you. If after all of that, he decides to leave, then you know it's over."

"You should have a talk show and market your How To Book because you always come up with these mind breaking ideas on how to get a man to cooperate."

"If I had that remedy, I wouldn't be single." They both laughed.

"Girl, what would I do without you?"

"Don't worry, because I'll always be here for you. You're like a sister to me."

Monica and Tracy's conversation was interrupted by a knock at the door. Monica started toward the door wondering who it could be. She looked through the peephole and was surprised to see Ms. Wilkens on the other end of the door. She glanced back at Tracy.

"It's Trey's mother. I wonder what she wants."

"Ms. Wilkens, what a pleasant surprise. What brings you by?" Monica asked, after opening the door.

"I need to talk to you. Can I come in?"

"Sure, please do."

Ms. Wilkens entered the condo and saw Tracy sitting on the sofa.

"Oh, hi Tracy. I'm sorry, am I interrupting something?"

"No not at all. As a matter of fact, I was just leaving," Tracy replied, figuring she'd give Monica and Ms. Wilkens a chance to talk. She gave Ms. Wilkens a hug before starting toward the door. "It was nice seeing you again, Ms. Wilkens. Monica, let me know how that thing turns out."

"Sure, I'll call you in the morning," Monica said, as both her and Ms. Wilkens took a seat on the sofa.

"I'm assuming that Trey isn't here?" Ms. Wilkens asked.

"No, he left heading to club about an hour ago."

"Good. That should give us time to talk."

Monica's mind started racing. She didn't have a clue what was so important that Ms. Wilkens couldn't have called.

"I'm sorry, where's my manners. Can I get you anything to drink?"

"No thank you, sweetheart."

"I hope you're not upset with me for not getting back to you about decorating your friend's nursery? It's just been really hectic lately."

"No, that's not why I'm here. I stopped by because I thought it was due time for me and my daughter-in-law to have a heart to heart. When we last talked you seemed rather upset. Is everything okay with you and Trey?"

Monica hesitates before responding. She didn't want to get into this with Trey's mother. "Everything is fine."

"Monica you don't have to pretend with me," Elaine replied, sensing Monica wasn't being totally honest with her.

After thinking about it, Monica decided to come clean. "Okay, the truth is that Trey and I are having problems. In fact, I'm considering leaving him."

"Things are that bad? I was afraid of this."

"Ms. Wilkens..." Monica replied before getting cut off.

"Honey please, call me Elaine."

"Okay. Elaine, Trey doesn't take his responsibility as a husband and father seriously. He stay out all night all the time without having the decency to call home or even check on his family. I'm beginning to think he miss the bachelor life. It makes me feel like he doesn't give a damn about me or his son."

Elaine understood all too well how Monica felt. She remembered the lonely nights and distance she dealt with from Kenneth.

"Honey, I know what you are going through. I've been there. Trey reminds me so much of his father. Kenneth did the same thing. Staying out all night and dared me to question where he'd been and who he was with."

Monica was surprised to hear how similar their lives were. She felt somewhat awkward to be discussing being a door mat for her husband with his mother.

"How did you deal with it?"

"Truthfully, I don't know. Sure, it hurt me to know that my husband was cheating on me, and he wasn't even trying to hide it. When I first found out, Trey was only three."

Monica thought to herself she could not imagine herself three years from now in this same situation.

"Why didn't you leave him?"

Elaine thought for a second, remembering the painful memories. "That was 27 years ago. I was scared and alone. Kenneth took care of me. I never had to work or want for nothing. I was so dependent on him that even if I wanted out, I had no way of taking care of the two of us. My family disowned me when I married Kenneth. Sweetheart, you are a beautiful, intelligent woman. As much as I love my son, I don't want you to limit yourself like I did."

"As I told him, I'm not putting up with his shit anymore. I love Trey with all my heart. I want my marriage, but I really don't know if it's worth all this heartache."

Monica glanced at the picture of the three of them as it sat on the night stand just to the left of Elaine. She noticed Monica staring at the picture.

"Baby, this is coming from the heart. The best thing you can do for Trey, yourself, and my beautiful grandson is to leave him if he doesn't change. If he really loves you he will do whatever it takes to keep you."

As she listened to Elaine she thought how ironic it was that their first mother and daughter talk would be about something so significant. Not to mention that her comments echoed Tracy suggestion.

"Elaine, can you do me a huge favor?"

"Sure just name it."

"Will you keep Junior tonight?"

"I would love to."

Monica explained to Elaine what she was planning to do. "Do you think he will choose his family?"

"Sugar, there's only one way to find out. Call him."

* * * * *

Trey was sitting at the bar swallowing down his third Rum and Coke when his cell phone rang. He placed the empty glass on bar counter before answering his phone.

"Hello?"

"Trey, can you please come home? I need to talk to you."

Trey figured Monica only wanted to finish their conversation from earlier.

"Can this wait?"

"No. Please, it's very important."

He thought about the letter from Candi and her request for him to give Monica a chance. "Alright, I'll be there in about twenty minutes."

Trey ended the call and placed the phone back in his jacket pocket. Meechi overheard Trey conversation and decided to pry.

"Are you leaving?"

"Yeah, I have to make a run. I'll be back in an hour."

Trey stepped away from the bar. He was a bit intrigued on what was so important that Monica couldn't discuss it over the phone.

"Don't forget... Tonight is the night we cut that deal with Big T," Meechi added as he had his own agenda for making sure Trey returned.

"How can I forget, I setup the meeting. Big T will be here around 10:30. I should be back by then."

Trey headed for the exit thinking it was due time for Meechi to find out that Trey knew he was the one that ordered the hit.

* * * * *

Trey entered the condo and started toward the bedroom. As he entered, Trey noticed the lights were dimmed and several candles were burning on both nightstands near the bed. "Monica," he called out.

"I'm in the bathroom. I'll be right out."

Trey removed his watch and bracelet. He laid them on the dresser. He saw the picture of himself, Junior and Monica. He remembered that particular photo was normally stationed on table in the living room. He stared at the photo for a moment. Deciding to check in on Junior, Trey headed to his room and looked in the bassinet only to discover Junior wasn't there.

"Where's my little man?"

"He's spending the night with your mother," Monica answered as she opened the door.

She stepped out of the bathroom wearing lingerie. She turned off the bathroom light and entered the bedroom, slowly approaching Trey. It had been awhile since they were intimate. Trey was still wondering what was so important that Monica demanded him to rush home. He momentarily became distracted as he got turned on watching Monica approach him.

"What's going on?" He asked, standing across the room with a hard-on.

"I thought we could use some time alone tonight."

Monica clapped her hands. The CD changer started playing R. Kelly's *Sex Me*. She continued to ease her way toward him, giving him a chance to appreciate her body. "Damn you're beautiful," he commented as she stood in front of him.

"Does that mean you like what you see?" Monica asked while reaching out for Trey's right hand, placing it on her chest.

"Definitely," he answered as he drew her close to him.

"Can you feel my heart pounding? It's racing for your love."

Trey thought about the meeting with Big T as he fantasized about having his way with his wife.

"Monica, I..." Monica placed her fingers over Trey lips silencing him.

"Tonight there will be no arguments, no business, and no problems. Just you and I, making love all night."

Trey embraced Monica as the two of them began kissing. Monica started undressing Trey, taking off his tie and unbuttoning his shirt.

"I want you so bad," Monica confessed as she kissed his chest.

Trey hoisted Monica into the air and gently laid her down on the bed.

* * * * *

The club lights dimmed as Kell's stepped onto the stage. He glanced at the crowd as the stage lights shined. He was standing before the audience dressed in an all-white suit, dress shoes and brim. He began singing acappella *Grinding* while all the women in the audience held on to every word. Couples start to gather around the stage slow dancing as Kell's continued to sing. Meanwhile, Meechi, Red and Tony were sitting at a table across from the bar.

"Meechi, do you really think we can pull this off?" Red asked as he sipped on a glass of cognac.

"Trust me. Tonight's the night. With Trey out of the way, Big T has to cut the deal with me."

"When are you going to tell us about the plan to get rid of Trey?"

"Relax, you'll both find out in due time."

Meechi spotted Shante entering the club and smiled. He picked up his glass of Ciroc, feeling untouchable as his plan began to shape up.

Red noticed Shante and his entourage making their way through the crowd.

"You're not going to believe who just walked in," Red whispered to Meechi as his eyes were locked in on Shante.

"Who," Tony responded.

"Donta's twin," he answered.

"Damn! That's all we need, some drama. Well, fuck it. They're in the wrong place," Tony added as he pulled out his phone to get some additional back-up.

Meechi stopped Tony from making the call. "Chill, I invited Shante. He's part of my plan."

"You're kidding, right?" Red asked in disbelief.

"Just relax. The both of you will understand momentarily."

Shante spotted Meechi, Red and Tony sitting at a table across from the bar. He approached the table with four of his men trailing him.

"Glad you could make it," Meechi said as he remained seated.

"Well don't start the party too soon. The only reason I'm here is to hear from you why you and Trey killed my brother."

"Please, have a seat. Can I get you anything?"

Shante reluctantly sat while his crew continued to stand. "The only thing you can get me is an explanation."

"I called you here to tell you face to face that I didn't have anything to do with what happened to your brother."

Shante pulled out a Philly Blunt and sniffed it before lighting the cigar. "Oh, is that a fact?" Shante responded.

"I told Trey that it would be a mistake to kill Donta, but you know Trey. He doesn't listen to anybody. He thought Donta was responsible for ambushing our drop this morning."

Shante continued to puff on his cigar while letting Meechi's words soak in. Finally, he placed the cigar down on the ashtray in front of him. "Forgive me for my disbelief. I seriously doubt you were against killing my brother. Regardless, I'm putting you and Trey on notice. You let Trey know that somewhere down the line, we will bump heads."

Red stood up from the table, not appreciating Shante's threat. Meechi motioned for him to rejoin him at the table. "Shante, I don't have any beef with you. What happened to your brother is between you and Trey. He will be arriving shortly. If anybody wanted to catch Trey slipping, this would be the perfect time to do it."

Shante was rather surprised at Meechi's suggestion. Despite not believing a word Meechi said, he was a bit curious to where Meechi was going with this.

"Why should I trust you? For all I know, this could be a setup."

Meechi reached inside his jacket and pulled out two envelopes. He slid them across the table toward Shante.

"I can give you a hundred thousand reasons why you can."

Shante glanced at Meechi, Red, and then Tony before picking up the envelopes. He opened them, one at a time. After looking over the money, he looked back at Meechi.

"What's the money for?"

"Let's just say it's my way of giving support to your cause. Fifty thousand now, and fifty more once he's dead."

Shante smiled as he picked up his cigar and took another puff. "I see we both share similar interest. Trey is about to meet his maker."

Tony and Red both grinned as they approved of Meechi's plan to use Shante to do their dirty work.

Melissa brought Meechi another drink. "Can I get any of you something to drink?"

"No thank you," Shante answered as he waited for her to leave the table.

"Tell me something Meechi, what exactly are you getting out of this?"

Meechi thought a second before responding. "I'll be getting rid of Trey." Meechi leaned in closer to Shante. "When you shoot him, make sure he's dead. The son of a bitch has more lives than a fuckin' cat."

*   *   *   *   *

Trey and Monica were under the sheets making love. Trey rolled over, and Monica climbed on top of him.

"I've missed you," she said before tonguing him.

CHAPTER 12

THE END IS NEAR

Across the street from Trey's condo sat Sgt. Turner in his car. He loaded his magazine clip into the gun as he continued to stare down the entrance of the building. Salivating over the chance to empty his gun in Trey's chest, Richard drifted back to last night's ambush. The gunshots continued to ring out over and over again in his mind. Seconds later, his mind flashed back to him standing over Ruth's corpse. His torturous image of his deceased wife only fueled the flames, as he felt like he could literally see himself shooting Trey.

"Trey, you son of a bitch. There's not a court in the world that's going to protect you from this execution waiting for you," Richard said to himself as he patiently waited for Trey to walk out the building.

*   *   *   *   *

Red, Meechi, and Tony were sitting at the table together after Shante and his entourage left.

"I've got to hand it to you Meechi, you sure know how to work the opposition," Red commented after appreciating how Meechi enticed Shante to kill Trey.

"Who, Shante? All he needed was a little encouragement so I gave it to him. After he gets rid of Trey, I'll kill him. I wouldn't want him to get it in his mind that he'll be the next King of the Streets, 'cause we all know, that will be me."

"Sounds like a plan coming together," Tony replied.

Meechi noticed Big T entering the club surrounded by five well-built guys in suits. Even with the flashy suits on, you could see their muscles bulging.

"Okay fellows, the fun is about to begin. Mr. West Coast himself just made his grand entrance."

Big T followed one of the club bouncers over to the table. Meechi practically jumped out of his seat to greet Big T.

"Glad you could make it," he said as he extended his hand out to shake Big T's hand.

"It looks like Trey knows how to run a club. Beautiful women and good entertainment," he commented after shaking Meechi's hand.

"Yes indeed, we keep the place packed."

"Trey mentioned that he's in the process of opening a second club in New York and wants to open a third in LA."

"That's the plan. Trey and I are currently in negotiations with a few investors regarding the possibility of developing a record label."

"Sounds like Trey is all about business. I have to admit, before actually seeing this place I was against it. But now, I think it might be doable in LA., providing we can get our business settled."

"I'm sure that won't be a problem," Meechi responded as he was anxiously waiting for the gunshots to sound off.

"Speaking of the guest of honor, where is Trey?" Big T asked.

Meechi was beginning to wonder the same thing. "He's probably running a few minutes late. Let me call him to be sure that he's en route."

Meechi noticed the concerned look on Red and Tony's face as he pulled out his phone to call Trey. After one ring, the call went straight to voicemail. Not knowing what to make of it, Meechi hung up.

"Well, where is he?"

"He has his cell phone turned off which is very odd. He never turns off his phone. Let me try to reach him at home," he added as he began sensing Big T getting impatient.

*   *   *   *   *

Trey and Monica were in the shower making love. Monica leaned her head back as the water from the shower head rushed down her chest.

"Baby, I love you. You mean the world to me and from this moment on, I'll make sure you know it. I know I haven't been a good husband to you, but I promise to change."

Monica was surprised but happy to hear Trey's revelation on how important she was to him. The telephone started ringing in the bedroom as Monica and Trey were still in the shower unaware. After several rings, the answering machine recording of Monica's voice played.

"Hi, you've reached the Wilkens residence. Sorry no one is available at this time. Please leave a detailed message and we will return your call at our earliest convenience. Have a blessed day."

Meechi waited until the beep before speaking. "Trey, its Meechi. If you're there pick up."

*   *   *   *   *

An hour later at the club, Meechi and Big T were still waiting for Trey. Meechi didn't have an answer for Big T. He knew Trey wanted to cut the deal, but he didn't have a clue to what was keeping him.

"What's the deal? Is he coming or not?"

"Honestly, I don't know. The last time I talked to him, he was heading home and was planning to be back for this meeting. I've tried to reach him at home and on his cell. This is unlike Trey. Something must have happened."

"Meechi, I don't know what kind of game you and Trey are playing, but I'm not amused. I thought Trey was a man of his word. He said he'd be here, but he's not."

Meechi was hoping the only reason Trey hadn't made it was because Shante and his men ambushed him outside the club. The only problem with that scenario was there was no gunfire. Meechi noticed Big T's wrestling lookalike body guards had made their way back to the table and were standing around him as the tension in his voice continued to grow.

"Do we really need Trey to be here? I can work this deal out with you and fill him in on it later."

Big T stood from the table with a disappointing expression. "Meechi, no disrespect intended. I flew in from California to cut this deal with Trey, not you. I don't like to be stood up or jerked around. I've been sitting here waiting on Trey for over an hour. When you hear from Trey, tell him I said he knows how to reach me. If he doesn't contact me by noon tomorrow, the deal is off."

Big T and his entourage exited the club. Minutes later, Shante approached the table.

"Who was the cat with them muscle-bound bodyguards?"

"Trouble with a capital T," Meechi said with a defeated look on his face. "I thought you said Trey was coming?"

"That's what we all thought," Red responded as he started to have doubts about Meechi's plan.

Shante dropped Meechi's money on the table. "Something ain't right about this shit, so I'm cutting my losses. If you want Trey dead, I suggest you do it yourself. I'm out," Shante informed before walking away.

Meechi turned the table over in frustration. "Damn! He screwed up everything. I can't even kill this fucker. As long as Trey is alive, Big T will never cut the deal with me."

Red knew there was need for concern as another one of Meechi plans was unsuccessful. "Do you think he's onto us?"

Trying to keep it together, Meechi thought for a second before answering. "As I said before, I don't give a fuck! At this point, I'm ready to go head to head with him. My father always said if you want something done right, it's best to do it yourself."

*   *   *   *   *

An hour later, Meechi's phone rang.

"Hello?" Meechi answered.

"I got your message. Is Big T still there?"

Meechi was surprised to finally hear from Trey after unsuccessfully making numerous attempts to reach him earlier.

"He left about two hours ago. What happened? I thought you said you would be here."

"Something important came up."

Meechi wanted to reach through the phone and choke Trey after hearing his nonchalant reply.

"That's it? Something came up? Big T is mad as hell. You almost blew the deal."

Unfazed by Meechi's comments regarding Big T's attitude, Trey continued with little concern.

"Fuck him. He'll get over it. He needs this deal more than I do. I can make my business happen with or without him. I'm sure he'll be willing to reschedule."

Meechi saw his chance and decided to go for it. "He's leaving tomorrow at noon. I tried to talk him into meeting us here in the morning but he refused. Big T wants to meet somewhere that won't attract cops."

"Is that so?" Trey responded.

"He agreed to meet us at the old abandoned warehouse downtown tomorrow morning at nine."

"Why would he agree to that? He doesn't know his way around Chicago. How in the hell is he supposed to find the warehouse?" Trey asked after realizing how odd that sounded.

"I'll have Red meet up with Big T and his entourage and escort them over to the warehouse in the morning."

"Okay, I'll see you and the fellows there in the morning," Trey added before hanging up.

Meechi noticed Red staring at him with a confused look on his face. "Meechi, what's wrong with you? You know Big T didn't agree to meet with us at that warehouse."

Meechi smiled with a sneaky grin on his face. "I know this, but Trey don't. When he step inside that warehouse tomorrow, the only way he'll make it out is in a body bag."

*   *   *   *   *

Trey was sitting on the edge of the bed with his phone in hand, contemplating his next move. He thought about how obvious this scheme of Meechi's was to him.

So you're ready to show your cards. Big T would never agree to meet anywhere with me that wasn't a public place. Well, like pops would say, let's getter done.

Monica walked up behind Trey and began to massage his shoulders. She noticed Trey in deep thought.

"Honey, did you get your meeting rescheduled?"

Thinking about how he was planning to counter Meechi's little trap, Trey hesitated before answering.

"Yeah, everything is taking care of."

"Good! Now let's go back to bed. You have some unfinished business to attend to."

*   *   *   *   *

Sgt. Turner was still sitting in his car waiting on Trey to come out. He began to get impatient after staking out Trey's condo for several hours.

"Fuck it! I'll just walk up to his door, ring the bell, and blow his ass away!"

As Sgt. Turner reached for his gun, his passenger car door opened and a man got in.

"What are you doing here? I almost shot you."

"I could ask you the same thing," Lt. Dawson responded. "Trying to stop you from making the biggest mistake of your life."

"William, we've already been through this. He has to pay for what he did."

"Richard, you can't kill this man based on speculation. You don't know if he was truly involved. We need to finish conducting our investigation."

"This is where my investigation leads me."

"Okay, then what?"

"Chicago will finally be free of the plague they call Trey, and I can pick up the few pieces left of my life."

"Richard, I can't pretend to know what you are feeling. But what I do know is you've been a respectable law enforcement officer to this city and community for well over twenty years. Don't let Trey take that away from you by turning you into him. A killer without a conscience. Besides, you have a young lady that needs you. I promised her I would find you."

William pulled out his cell phone and pushed recent calls and selected the last call before handing the phone to Richard.

"Hello."

"Katie, hi sweetheart," Richard replied after being caught off guard.

Katie, Richard's daughter, was away attending college at Florida State University. She hadn't been home since spring break.

"Daddy, hi! I finally tracked you down. I've been trying to reach you for hours. I kept getting your voicemail."

"I'm sorry honey. I think my battery is dead."

"I heard about Mom. Why didn't you call me?"

Richard was surprised that Katie had already heard about the shooting. He felt awful that during his quest for vengeance, he had forgotten to call her. "Honey, I was planning to call you tomorrow. Honestly, I didn't know how to tell you. How did you find out about the shooting?"

"My roommate at the dorm saw a news report online and told me. When I read it, I called you. After I couldn't reach you I called the precinct, and they patched me through to William."

"Have you caught the guys responsible for this yet?"

"Not yet, but I will."

"Dad, can you come pick me up? I just arrived at the airport. I'm heading down to baggage claim."

Richard was stunned to hear Katie was in Chicago. "Sure, why did you catch such a late flight?"

"It was last minute and I didn't want to wait until tomorrow."

"Okay I'm leaving now. I will be there in fifteen minutes."

"Good, that should give me enough time to collect my luggage. I love you, Dad."

"I love you too sweetheart," he answered before hanging up.

Richard stared at William before tossing him his phone. "Well done, you've made your point. I will take a step back and see this investigation through. If I find out that Trey was behind my wife's shooting, I will be his judge, jury and executioner."

"Fair enough. Now go pick up Katie and spend some much needed time with your daughter. Leave the heavy lifting of this investigation to me. I promise you I will find the guys responsible."

"Thank you my friend. I need this more than anything."

"I know," William added before climbing out of the car. He watched Richard drive away.

CHAPTER 13

IT'S KILL OR BE KILLED

The next morning, the clock read 6:30 a.m. when Monica rolled over and noticed Trey wasn't lying next to her.

"Trey," she called out as she sat up in bed.

Trey walked out of the bathroom, attempting to put on his tie.

"I'm still here, baby. I wasn't going to leave without saying goodbye."

After tightening his tie, Trey slipped on his jacket before sitting on the bed next to her. He placed his left hand on her thigh.

"What time will you be back?"

"I'm not sure, possibly around noon. After I see this meeting through today, I promise it'll be you, me and Trey Jr."

Monica kissed him feeling good about the sudden change in their relationship. "I love you."

"Baby, if for some reason I don't make it back home, I want you to have this."

Trey reached under the bed and pulled out a black briefcase.

"Trey that's the first time I ever heard you say that. Now I'm worried."

"Baby, don't be. Everything will be fine. I just want to make sure I have all my ducks in a row. Go ahead, open the briefcase."

Monica opened the briefcase. She saw several keys, property deeds, stocks & bond certificates, and a couple of bank books from several banks.

"The keys are to my safe deposit boxes. Everything you need to access my personal accounts are in this briefcase. I have to go. I will see you later," Trey added before kissing her on the lips.

Trey walked out of the bedroom and started toward the front door. He grabbed his keys off the nightstand. He looked down at the picture of him and his family. He picked it up and kissed it before placing it back and exiting the condo. Monica was still sitting in the bed with the black briefcase between her legs. She filtered through all the documents inside the briefcase while crying. She knew if Trey was concerned enough to give her access to all of his accounts, then there was a great possibility that he may not return.

*   *   *   *   *

Meechi, Red, and Tony entered the warehouse with three men from Donta's crew. The warehouse was totally dark.

"I know he's here, his car is out front," Red said as he searched for the light switch.

"Hit the light switch, it's over there on the wall," Meechi instructed Tony as he pointed just to the right of Red.

Tony turned on the lights, but only a portion of the warehouse came on. The six of them spotted Trey standing across from them on the other side of the warehouse with limited lighting.

"Where's Big T?"

"Good question. Maybe he's returning the favor from last night."

Trey stared at Meechi for a second before responding. "Meechi, what is this really about? Big T would never agree to meet with me anywhere that isn't a public place. Besides, I met with him earlier at his hotel suite."

Meechi grinned, knowing that he was busted. "It seems as if I outsmarted myself. The truth is, we're unhappy with the way you've been running this organization lately. So we decided it was time for a change."

Trey slowly reached inside his jacket pocket and pulled out a pack of Black & Milds with his engraved lighter. As he did, Meechi and his entourage watched closely as they were anticipating Trey making a move.

"We? Are you referring to the six of y'all or just you?"

"All of us," Meechi responded.

"So let me guess. You think you're the man to take over?"

Meechi's confident body language pretty much answered Trey's question. "Correction, I've already taking over. The only loose end is you," Meechi answered.

Trey took another puff from his cigar before responding. "I'm impressed. I see you've thought this out down to the last detail. The truth finally surfaces. It seems as if you want to be me. So tell me one thing, why did you rob me and frame Donta?"

Meechi figured since everything was out in the open he had nothing to hide. "Donta was weak. I would have killed him myself but that would have defeated the purpose. You see, I needed a believable alibi for your death."

Trey took another hit from the cigar before dropping it to the ground.

"I have to admit, it was a pretty slick plan. I probably would not have figured out your scheme if you hadn't sent them two flunkies to do your dirty work."

Sarcastically, Meechi clapped. "Well, well, well. It seems like you've done your homework."

Trey's facial expression changed as he remembered how Harold betrayed his father. "Why? Of all people, how could you betray me?"

Meechi laughed thinking how naive Trey was for not seeing this coming.

"Allow me to borrow one of you quotes. This is business, nothing personal. Lately you've been slipping. We could have expanded to the West Coast. But The Great Trey Wilkens doesn't have the balls to take down Big T. The old Trey wouldn't hesitate to wax his ass."

"I don't have balls you say? This is coming from someone who wasn't man enough to handle his own business. Instead you pay some low level flunkies who ratted you out the first chance they got. You've ridden my coat tail for all these years. I trusted you, but obviously you had other plans. It's been said that once a dog runs a stray, he must be put down."

"Wow, I'm a dog? I guess I'm the big dog in this yard. It's always been about me, not you. Without me you'd be nothing! For years, I've dreamed about the day of burying you next to your father," Meechi said with a cocky demeanor.

Trey tried not to show how much Meechi comment touched a nerve.

"Is that a fact? So you tricked me into meeting you here with plans of killing me.

I bet your crew had no idea that today you would be leading them to their death."

"Trey, who are you kidding? You're done. I'm the New King. Nobody's afraid of you anymore."

"You know the funny thing about all of this? If you hadn't sent Derek and Terrell to kill me yesterday, you would be the man. I had decided to step down and help you take over."

"Nevertheless, this will be even more rewarding to know that I was the man to dethrone you," Meechi answered.

As Meechi continued to run his mouth, Red began to wonder why Trey would be standing there alone so calm and confident. It just didn't add up. Knowing how calculating and prepared Trey normally was, catching him off guard just seemed too good to be true.

"I'm afraid I'm going to have to put your dreams on a permanent hiatus."

"Unless you learned something different in school, six against one is a no win ratio."

Trey snapped his fingers signaling someone to turn on the secondary lights. Meechi and his entourage were in a state of shock to see twelve men with guns pointed at them. Meechi's heart literally skipped a beat when he saw Shante step out from the crowd of men standing beside Trey.

"What the fuck is this? Shante what the hell are you doing?"

"It's like you said, this is business not personal. Trey made me an offer that I simply could not refuse. You're looking at the new era to the Midwest, my friend."

Meechi was furious. He got played by both Shante and Trey.

"Is this some kind of sick joke? Shante, this man killed your brother!"

"Yes, and you set my brother up to be killed. For that you deserve everything you got coming."

Meechi realized he had burned himself when Trey coerced him into confessing his entire scheme.

"Trey, you son of a bitch!"

"I would stay and chat but I don't want to get blood on my suit," Trey said smiling before walking away.

It dawned on Meechi that he allowed Trey to bait him into setting himself up. He wanted to be rid of Trey so bad that he didn't carefully think his plan through. In frustration, Meechi reached for his gun.

"Meechi no!" Tony yelled trying to protect Meechi as Trey's entourage started firing. Tony was shot several times as he was unable to avoid the round of bullets.

*   *   *   *   *

Exiting the warehouse, Trey could hear the gunshots as he started toward his car. As he opened his car door, his driver side mirror was shot off. The bullet missed him by inches. Trey pulled his gun and quickly turned around. Aiming in the direction the shot came, he saw Meechi limping toward him. Bleeding from bullet wounds to the chest and leg, Meechi squeezed his trigger again but was out of bullets.

"That's the third time you missed and the last time. Game over."

Trey fired his gun. The bullet hit Meechi directly in the temple. Meechi fell to the ground, dying on impact. Trey looked at Meechi's body as it lay motionless.

Tray heard footsteps and turned and faced Sgt. Turner who was pointing his gun at him.

"Drop the gun, Trey."

"Good work, Detective. You think you've finally caught me with my hand in the cookie jar? I know you witnessed the entire thing. It was self-defense."

"Trey, I will only say this once more, drop the gun."

Trey dropped his gun and raised his hands in the air. Sgt. Turner remained cautious, not expecting Trey to surrender so easily. Truthfully, he wanted a reason to empty his clip in Trey.

"Is this how you treat all of your friends?"

"Only the ones who back stab me and try to kill me. Enough with the friendly discussion cop, bring on the handcuffs," Trey replied as he held out his arms preparing to be handcuffed.

"Arresting you would be too good for you. The other night, you sent your goons to kill me. Instead they killed my wife. You took my son, my wife, basically my entire life. I think it's time for me to do society a favor," Sgt. Turner said before cocking his gun. "Richie, I know we got history with your son and all, but I don't know what you're talking about. I didn't send anyone after you or your wife."

"You can't lie your way out of this."

Sgt. Turner suddenly felt a gun barrel pushed against the back of his head. "He's not lying. I sent those guys to kill you. Now drop your gun and turn around slowly," the gunman warned before taking a few steps back.

Richard dropped his gun at the gunman's request before turning to face him.

"This is good. Almost too good to be true," Trey added after feeling a bit relieved that William showed up when he did. He stooped down and picks up the gun.

"William, why?" Richard asked.

"You know the answer to that, money. Trey's offer was too tempting to refuse."

"I'm glad you showed when you did. I'm not so sure Richie was planning to do this one by the book," Trey said to William.

"Trey, I think you better leave. Richard called for backup."

"So, you decided to make a deal with the devil?"

"As they say, cash rules everything around you."

"So you're responsible for my wife's death?"

"Actually, you're responsible. You got too close for your own good. That bullet was meant for you, not Ruth."

"You bastard!" Richard charged William.

He grabbed William by the throat with one hand and the gun with the other. Richard wrestled William to the ground managing to knock the gun out of William's hand. Both men were on the ground struggling to gain possession of the gun. William gained the advantage and picked up the gun attempting to aim it at Richard. Richard continued to tussle with William, trying to get the gun away from him. As the gun was lowered between the two, a gunshot echoed as Trey looked on.

Richard was the first to react, realizing that he had been shot in the stomach. He released his grip from the gun. William kept the gun pointed at Richard as he stood up. "I'm sorry my friend, but our partnership has been dissolved," William added as he stood over Richard.

He squeezed the trigger, firing another shot for good measure.

"Damn! That was cold. You killed your own partner," Trey said as he witnessed the entire thing.

"So did you," William replied.

"Mine deserved it," Trey answered while hiding the gun behind his back.

William put his gun away and began dusting off his suit. "He fucked up a good suit. You know you're going to owe me for this."

"Yeah, I was afraid of that," Trey replied. He pointed the gun at William and fired two shots to the chest. William fell to the ground in disbelief.

"Consider my debt paid. I forgot to mention I don't trust cops, especially dirty ones."

Trey shot him a third time in the chest. He picked up the driver-side mirror and opened the trunk of his car. He tossed the mirror in the trunk and grabbed the black briefcase. He walked up to Sgt. Turner and Lt. Dawson bodies and laid the briefcase near William's hand. Trey wiped the gun he used to shoot William and placed it in Richard's hand. He could hear sirens as he rushed to his car and drove away.

CHAPTER 14

LIFE AFTER DEATH

A month later, Trey and Monica were in Los Angeles for the opening of his new nightclub. Trey stood on the stage with West Coaster Rapper Great Dane.

"I would like to personally thank everyone for coming out to the opening of Trey's Nightclub. I have to say tonight will be a night to remember. My good friend and newly signed recording artist to Hustlin' Entertainment, Great Dane will kick off the festivities." Both men hugged before Great Dane began performing.

Monica finally had the life she wanted. Trey had given up his life of crime. He kept his word and helped Shante take over. She felt she owed this second chance to Tracy and Ms. Wilkens.

"Well sweetheart, what do you think?" Trey asked after kissing her on the cheek.

"I love it."

Trey and Monica went over to the VIP section and took a seat at one of the tables.

"I think it's time for us to find a place out here."

Monica was surprised that Trey was considering leaving Chicago. "Are you serious?"

"Yes. I've already arranged for us to meet with a realtor first thing Monday morning to begin our search for a new home."

"What about your mother?"

"I was hoping you would help me convince her to move to LA with us."

"Sure, but what about the club in Chicago?"

"Don't worry baby, the club will take care of itself. Shante can run the club. Chicago will always be home, but for us we need a new beginning."

Monica was excited. She felt as if God finally was answering her prayers.

"Trey, I love you so much."

"I love you too. Why don't you call your mother in law and give her the good news. I'll be right back, I need to check on the bartenders."

Trey left the table and approached the bar. "How is everything going?" Trey asked Marvin.

"We're doing good, boss. This place is packed. I know one thing, everybody is raving about A Glass Full of Sin."

"Glad to hear my drink is getting popular on the West Coast," Trey replied before walking away.

Unnoticed by Trey, Katie, Sgt. Turner's daughter, entered the club and spotted Trey as he was heading to the restroom. She made her way through the crowd as they were vibing with Great Dane's performance. Katie followed Trey into the men's room. She locked the bathroom door behind her. Standing several feet away from Trey, she reached into her jacket and pulled out a chrome nickel plated .45 Colt.

Trey heard the door latch and turned around. He faced Katie as she pointed the .45 Colt at him.

"Why did you kill my parents?" Katie asked.

Her hands were trembling, and Trey knew his back was against the wall. He had his gun on him, but didn't want to make a move to provoke her to shoot.

"Katie, take it easy. Don't shoot. You don't need a gun to talk to me."

"Answer me! Why did you do this?"

"I did not kill your parents."

"Liar!" Katie shouted. She fired a shot into the urinal wall.

"Okay, calm down. You don't need to do this."

"When my father accused you of killing Ricky, I always thought my Dad blamed you for his death because of your reputation. Now I know the truth. You are exactly what he said you were, a cold hearted killer. You killed my brother, mother and my father. You never gave a damn about nobody besides yourself."

"Katie, please listen to me."

"No you listen! I can't believe I allowed myself to ever fall in love with you. I hate you!" Trey knew Katie was looking for revenge. He wasn't surprise that she blamed him despite feeling she should own some fault to how things turned out.

"Katie, you know the real reason Ricky got killed. Your brother came to my club and pulled a gun on me. What were my men supposed to do? Their job was to protect me. The truth of the matter was Ricky couldn't accept the fact that a black guy was fucking his sister. Now, if you really want to kill me go ahead, but it won't solve shit because I didn't kill your parents. Your father's partner deserves the credit for that."

Katie fired a second shot after hearing Trey blame William for her parent's death.

"Lie again and the next bullet will be in your chest."

"It's the truth."

"You expect me to believe that William killed my mom and dad then shot himself three times. How stupid do you think I am?"

"It didn't exactly happen in that order. William was on my payroll. I was paying him to keep your father off my trail. He paid a couple of guys to take out your father. During a shootout with your father, your mom was shot. These men did not work for me. I had nothing to do with this. I actually didn't know William was involved in the shooting until he admitted it to your father. Your dad approached me and accused me of killing your mom. I told him just like I'm telling you I had nothing to do with it. That's when William appeared and the two got into a scuffle. William shot your father during the struggle for his gun."

Katie lowered her gun as she considered the theory. "Why would he do this? He was his partner."

"He was protecting his investment. Without me, there is no under the table payoff."

"If what you say is true who shot William?"

"I did, but only to protect myself. Seeing him with that gun in hand after killing your father made me realize he was going to kill me as well. He told me I owed him, and he was planning on collecting. Besides, I witnessed the entire thing and he could not afford to let me live."

"Why should I believe you?"

"Like I said before, it's the truth. I can take some responsibility for how things unfolded, but don't ruin your life by trying to finish what your father started. You're not a killer." Katie tried to keep her emotions in check but she couldn't. She broke down into tears. "Trey, no matter how you slice this up, it's all your fault. If it wasn't for you I would still have a family."

"Someday, I will have to pay for my past whether it's now or later, but why should you be the one to throw away your life to take mine? Your father's obsession to make me pay for Ricky's death cost him and your mom their life. Let's end this now."

Trey carefully started toward Katie.

"I can't!" Katie replied as she aimed the gun at Trey.

"Katie, I'm going to move slowly. Give me the gun," Trey asked as he carefully made his way toward her.

Standing in front of Katie, Trey held his hand out hoping that she would surrender the gun. Katie reluctantly hands him the gun.

"What do I do now? I'm all alone," she asked as she hugged Trey for comfort while continuing to cry.

"Take one day at a time. Katie, you're not alone. I'll always be here for you. If you ever need anything, let me know."

After finally pulling herself together, Katie kissed Trey on the lips before drawing back. She unbuttoned her blouse and revealed the wire. Katie looked him directly in the eyes.

"What I want, you can't give me back. My family," Katie added as she steps away from him.

"Bravo, nice performance. You were actually believable," Trey responded as he watched Katie unlock the door and exit the restroom.

Two federal agents entered the restroom and handcuffed Trey. As he was being escorted out of the club, he saw the devastated look on Monica's face. His new life was short-lived.

For Monica, this was more than just a normal disappointment. She felt embarrassed and hurt at the same time. After all she had endured over the years, the drug dealing, the killing and the cheating, Monica finally came to the realization that the dream she had of having a normal life with Trey was just that, a dream. No matter how much Trey may want to change, he would never be free of his King of the Streets persona. His dealings seemed to always find a way to interfere with their happiness.

Monica stood outside the club as Trey was shoved in to the squad car. "This is where the pain ends," Monica said to herself as she watched the federal agents climb into the car and drive off with Trey. For the first time in their marriage, Trey was leaving her, and she hoped that he wouldn't return.

CHAPTER 15

REVELATIONS

Trey was being ushered past the television crews at the Greenville Correctional facility. Special Agent Lora Crowne uncuffed Trey and released him into the custody of the correctional facility.

"It's too bad. I was just getting use to your scent. Maybe once I'm cleared of these ridiculous charges, you and I can do dinner."

"Trust me, you will have your hands full trying not to become another Greenville statistic. I hear these inmates can be rather forceful."

The other two agents found humor in Lora's comments.

"Sweetheart, Trey Wilkens never has to worry. Believe me when I tell you, I can take care myself. I only hope that you won't be lying in bed at night worrying about me, wishing and thinking about what could have been."

"Sorry, but I don't date criminals," Lora replied.

"Alright Romeo, I've heard enough of your poetic bullshit," Special Agent Kendricks said as he intervened.

"Well, it appears your partner has the hots for you. My bad homie, I didn't know you were trying to hit that. Don't hate if she chooses The King of the Streets. Honestly, can you blame her?"

"You are so sure of yourself, you low budget Pacino wanna be. You will regret your actions after spending a few weeks behind these walls."

"The only thing I'm regretting is the fact that I don't have any Tic Tacs on me. Your breath is burning my eyebrows."

"Mister Funny Man, let me cut right through the shit! It would give me great pleasure to see you strapped to a chair. You killed Sgt. Turner, an outstanding law enforcement officer, and Lt. Dawson who was a personal friend of mine. For that, you can bank on me making sure you get everything you deserve."

"Really, Lt. Dawson was a personal friend. Well then I guess much like him, you're on the take."

"What the hell are you insinuating?"

"Don't pretend to be oblivious to this. Dirty cops usually flock together. So now I understand, this is personal."

"Arresting and bringing you to justice for the crimes you committed is business and done by the book. Seeing you executed for murdering two highly decorated officers is business and personal."

"Your friend was dirty and a killer, but the real reason you are leading this investigation is to have me take the fall for your crooked-ass friend. I've seen this story play out before. You are simply a badge with an agenda. If you haven't taken notes from Sgt. Turner's memoirs, you should remember to never throw salt at the King's feet."

"That's amusing that you would refer to yourself as a King. Well, I don't speak Ebonics so excuse me for my ignorance. Since I have the pleasure of being in the company of royalty, I would like to inform Your Highness that your throne awaits," Agent Kendricks replied as he turned to walk away. "By the way, you can bank on me making sure you get everything due to you."

"Get this clown processed and locked up immediately," Special Agent Kendricks yelled, not amused by Trey's condescending remarks.

* * * * *

Monica heard a knock at the door. She opened it and welcomed Pastor Thomas into her home. "Thank you for coming Pastor Thomas. With my husband's case all over the news, I'm embarrassed to even show my face in church."

"Sister Wilkens, I was glad to hear from you. I understand what you are going through and know that it has to be a difficult time for you and your family. I must say, don't ever feel ashamed to come to God's house. Our heavenly Father is a forgiving Lord and loves you unconditionally. After all, you are not the one on trial."

"I know, but why do I feel partially responsible for my husband's crimes? I knew from the day I married him our indifferences would eventually cause problems in our relationship."

"Sister Wilkens, standing by your husband even during the most horrific times is what love is truly about. However, I have serious concerns regarding this union. Sister Wilkens, forgive me for saying, but I truly believe you can do so much better. It appears as if Satan has a hold on him, but his soul can be saved. He has to truly want to know God. I must say while I respect your loyalty to your marriage, you cannot serve the Lord full-heartedly if you are sleeping with the enemy."

Monica let Pastor Thomas's words soak in as she knew he was right. "I must have been crazy to stay with him this long."

"Your husband and I believe it or not were best friends as teenagers growing up. We lived on the same street and hung out together. Trey was one of the nicest kids you could ever know. He would share his last with you and was a true friend. The one thing I remember most about Trey is how much he adored his father. The day his father was killed changed him forever."

"Well thank God for the different path you chose. You are a pastor, devoting your life to saving souls while he is taking lives. Maybe he could use some spiritual guidance."

"I don't know this Trey. I've tried to reach out to him in the past. He became defensive and has never returned to the church since. I do believe that deep down inside there is a young boy crying to get out."

"Please Pastor Thomas, Trey was making great strides with turning over a new leaf before all of this transpired. While I don't feel our marriage will survive, my son needs his father."

"For you and your son, I will see what I can do. If Trey truly want to make a change for the better and build a relationship with the Lord, I would be honored to show him the way."

CHAPTER 16

DOMINANCE AT RISK

Trey was in his cell working out. He was doing sit ups when his lawyer walked into his cell accompanied by a guard.

"Wilkens, you have a visitor."

"Ashcroft, when are you getting me out of this joint?"

"I go before the judge tomorrow to see if we can get bail set."

"What are the chances of us beating this case?"

"Trey, they have some incriminating evidence against you."

"Yeah, I'm sure but my hands were forced. They have no murder weapon to tie me to the murders."

"Your confession hurt our case substantially."

"How was I supposed to know Katie was wired? Hell, she held me at gun point and fired two shots. Besides, I only admitted to shooting Lt. Dawson which I stated was self-defense."

"I'm laying a defense for that."

"Good, because you better win this case."

"Don't I always win?"

"Right now that's not all that comforting to me considering the situation. I'm locked down in this hell hole wearing this colorful ass jump suit. I don't intend on being in here much longer. Hurry the hell up and get me out of here."

"I will."

* * * * *

Monica was at home holding the baby watching television when the news aired the coverage of Trey's arrest.

"Hi, I'm Angela Stewart reporting live from Greenville Correctional facility where the attorney of suspected Drug Lord, Trey Wilkens, is currently visiting his client."

Ashcroft made his way through the crowd with camera crews in his face as he attempted to get back to his vehicle. *"Mr. Ashcroft, can I get your comment on the state of your client at this point?"* Angela Stewart asked.

"No comment at this time," he answered as he walked off, attempting to inch closer towards his vehicle. The reporter faced the camera. *"Trey Wilkens is currently being indicted for the murders of Lt. Dawson and Sgt. Turner, along with the death of six other men killed during an undercover drug raid that recovered over ten kilos of cocaine. Chicago's King of the Streets was surprisingly out-smarted by the late Sgt. Turner's daughter, Katie Turner. Sources say she was able to get him to confess to the involvement in the murders."* Monica turned off the television as she continued to rock her son to sleep.

"God, please tell me what to do? I love Trey so much, but I can't continue to be part of this roller coaster ride."

* * * * *

Trey was in the correctional facility's workout area lifting weights. As he loaded weights on the barbell, three other inmates entered the workout area. The fourth inmate distracted and attacked the guard at the gate assigned to guard Trey. Rendering him unconscious, he joined the other inmates.

Trey noticed the forth inmate joining them, holding the guard's baton in hand.

"While I appreciate the welcoming party, I'm in the middle of a workout," Trey said before placing an additional ten pound weight on the barbell.

"Hold on, Mr. King of the Streets. You might run the streets, but in Greenville, I run this shit. So you show me some fuckin' respect. In here, it's Deek's world. You got that?"

"All right, Deek, you're the man in here. Well as a visitor, I'd like to make a request."

"A request, this should to be good. I'm listening."

"I'm simply asking for you to give me a pass."

"Why should I do that?"

"Look fellows, let's just say this is the wrong place wrong time for this shit. You really don't want to do this. So, why don't you guys turn around and we can all forget this little impromptu ever took place."

"Wow! What a request. Unfortunately, my friend, I have a little problem with your request. Let's say we really want to do this? What can you do about it, shoot us?"

"If I wanted you dead you would be."

"Oh, I think you forgot that we're not on the streets. Greenville don't let you carry gats so you're on your own, partner."

"Deek, this is real talk. I was hoping we could avoid this whole ambush thing."

"I'm sure you would, but it's not your call to make. It's time for a new

King of the Streets. Your time is up. Before things get fatal, I need to deliver a message. My cousin Shante sends his regards."

"I'm sure I'll get the opportunity to thank him personally. It's obvious that you weren't listening. I'm a second degree black belt, so unless you got a couple more guys coming to the party, you really don't want to do this."

"Man fuck this, talking is over," Chris, one of the other three inmates, yelled as he charged Trey.

Trey met Chris with a barbell weight across the skull. He quickly side stepped Deek and thrust kicked inmate three in the throat. Rico charged Trey with the baton. Deek grabbed Trey from behind. Trey kicked the baton out of Rico's hand. Rico hit Trey in the stomach three times, and once across the face.

Trey finally broke free from Deek's grip. He threw an elbow to his jaw and ducked under a punch that landed on Deek's face. Rico was shocked that he hit Deek instead of Trey, sending him to the floor. Trey unloaded on Rico with a series of punches, a knee thrust to the face and a round house to put him down. He turned around and Deek was getting off the floor.

"I guess you're no longer the man," Trey said as he delivered a spinning back kick to Deek's jaw, knocking him out cold.

"Looks like I've had my work out for the day," Trey said, smiling as he left the workout area.

*　　*　　*　　*　　*

The next morning, Trey was being escorted to one of the inmate visitor rooms. He was surprised to see Monica inside waiting for him.

"You have ten minutes," the guard said.

"Baby, I was hoping you would come to see me. Once I get released, I intend on fulfilling my promise of working on our future."

"Trey, we have no future together. I only came to tell you I can't do this anymore. I've decided to file for a divorce."

Trey felt like someone had just dropped a ton of bricks on him. "Monica, we can work this out. I know being my wife has not been easy. I promise if you give me the chance to make things right..."

"Trey, you are in prison currently being indicted for the murders of two police offers and the death of six men in relation to drugs. They are calling you an animal and already talking about the death penalty. Do you have any idea what this is doing to me and your mother?"

"Monica, my lawyer is working to get these charges dropped."

"I can't say I'm surprised. Even as good as Walter is, this isn't going away no time soon. Trey, I love you more than you will ever know. But, I am truly tired of this life and feel this is best for me and our son."

Tears began to trickle down her cheeks as she put her right hand on his face. "Monica, listen to me," Trey pled.

"Goodbye, Trey," Monica said as she turned to walk away. "Can you at least give me a proper goodbye?" Trey asked, grabbing her by the arm.

Monica turned and kissed Trey passionately before walking away.

"Monica, I will make this right. I will not give up on us."

Tears flowed down Monica's caramel cheeks as she exited the room.

*   *   *   *   *

Ashcroft and the District Attorney were meeting with Judge Waters at Trey's bail hearing.

"Your Honor, my client is not a flight risk and should be released on bail to stand trial."

"Your Honor, the people ask for remand due to Mr. Wilkens' history of violence which makes him a threat to society."

"If I may Your Honor, despite my client's popularity with Chicago's finest, he has no priors. Due to the severity of the charges against my client, I'm deeply concerned for his safety. I can provide adequate security for my client while he stands trial against the allegations."

"Mr. Ashcroft, I'm going the grant bail for your client at the sum of one million dollars under the condition that he releases his passport."

"Your Honor, at this time I would like to put a notice of motion for evidence exhibit 12436 tape recording to be deemed inadmissible for trial."

"What is your justification for this motion?" Judge Waters asked.

"Your Honor, the key witness working with the federal authorities held my client at gun point in a men's restroom and threatened to kill him unless he confessed to the murders in question. She fired two shots at my client forcing him to confess to the involvement of the murders only to save his own life. Therefore, this evidence was coerced and illegally obtained."

"Your Honor, the recording, along with the witness testimony is key evidence that not only puts the defendant at the scene of the crime but also has his confession to the involvement of the murders of two officers. The defendant was never in any real danger. Federal agents were on the other side of the door," the prosecuting attorney added.

Judge Waters read the evidence documents while listening to the prosecutor plead her case to use the evidence.

"Unfortunately, I cannot allow the recording to be used during the trial because it was illegally obtained. The jury selection will begin at 10:00am tomorrow morning. I expect the two of you to plead this case without making a circus act in my court room."

*   *   *   *   *

Despite Shante and Trey's truce over a month ago, Shante couldn't pass up the opportunity to have Trey taken out. This would officially crown him the new King of the Streets and give him payback for his brother's death.

Shante was standing outside of Trey's club, smoking a cigarette and thinking about the news Cortez had given him.

"So let me get this straight, four guys and none of them could get the job done?"

"This is straight from Deek. Man, two of his guys got concussions, the third has a broken trachea, and he broke Deek's jaw."

Shante was fuming. "Damn! What the fuck happened? I should be celebrating Trey ass lying in the county morgue but instead, this mutha-fucka is getting the last laugh."

"Shante, it gets worse. Trey knows you sent them to take him out."

"Well then let the games begin. Come on, let's head inside. I better get my party on tonight because tomorrow, I got to figure out how to get the job done."

As Shante dropped the cigarette butt, he saw a black Escalade pull up and doors fly open. Two men with guns pointed at Shante grabbed him, forcing him into the Escalade. Cortez attempted to save Shante and took a bullet in the head for his troubles.

∗   ∗   ∗   ∗   ∗

Tuesday morning, Trey heard a knock at his hotel room door as he was dressing for court. Ashcroft arrived to advise him what to expect.

"So is Katie still expected to testify?"

"I sure hope so," Ashcroft replied as he straightened Trey's tie.

"Man, this is my livelihood. I need you to come through for me today."

"Trey, I will do my best, this you know. I really feel we can win this case."

"Well, let's not keep my audience waiting," Trey replied.

He opened the room door and Candi, was waiting in the hallway.

"Hi handsome, I wanted to come by to give you a supporting hug and wish you well."

"Come in," Trey replied after hugging her.

"You really need to reconsider letting me provide security for you until the trial is over."

"I have all the protection I need. My men will not let anyone get through that poses a threat. Can you give me a minute?"

"Sure, I will meet you in the lobby," Ashcroft replied as he left the room.

"Trey, I wish I could be in the court room with you today but I know your wife will be at your side."

"I doubt it, but all the same, it would be best if you didn't. I better head down. Meet me back here after court. Maybe we can do dinner."

"Sure, I'd like that."

*   *   *   *   *

The jury had been selected, and Nina, the prosecuting attorney, was stating her case. She completed questioning Katie on the wittiness stand. "Your witness," Nina stated as she took her seat.

Ashcroft approached. "Ms. Turner, you stated that my client confessed to murdering Lt. Dawson, is that correct?"

"Yes, that's correct."

"Ms. Turner, are you the daughter of the late Sgt. Turner?"

"Yes."

"Ms. Turner, have you ever been intimately involved with the defendant?"

Katie hesitated before answering the question.

"Objection, Your Honor," District Attorney Nina yelled after being caught off guard regarding the allegation of a possible relationship between Katie and the defendant. "Overruled. Kate, please answer the question."

"Yes."

"Isn't it true that during your relationship with the defendant, you told him that your father hated him because he knew you were in love with him?"

"Objection!" Nina yelled again.

"Overruled," the judge responded.

"Yes, but..."

"Katie, isn't it also true that your father blamed the defendant for your brother's death?"

"Objection, Your Honor, he is badgering the witness."

"Overruled," the judge replied.

"Yes, he believed Trey was responsible."

"Is it true that my client broke your heart when he dumped you for another woman?"

"No."

"Ms. Turner, remember you are under oath. Isn't it true that the reason you agreed to aid the federal authorities with this case is because you blame yourself for your father's death?"

"No."

"Your father was so fixated on my client because of your involvement with him that it caused him his life?"

"No."

"Objection!" Nina yelled again.

"Sustained. Counselor, redirect and get to the point."

"Okay. Katie, did you go to my client's club in California, follow him into the rest room, lock the door, and hold him by gun point while threating to kill him unless he confessed to killing your father?"

Katie refused to answer. "Ms. Turner, answer the question," the judge replied.

"Yes."

"Isn't it also true that you are still in love with my client?"

"Objection, Your Honor!"

"Overruled. Ms. Turner, answer the question."

"Yes, I loved him with all my heart, but it wasn't enough. My relationship with Trey cost me my entire family. Now I'm all alone. I have nothing left," she answered, literally in tears.

"No further questions, Your Honor. I believe my work here is done."

*   *   *   *   *

"Trey, thanks for dinner. It was unfortunate that we were bombarded by reporters though," Candi said as she took off her heels.

"I especially liked the hot little number from Channel 6 asking you if you are my mistress."

"I'm sure she didn't appreciate you throwing wine on her white dress."

"I offered to pay her cleaning bill. Speaking of dresses, let me help you get out of this one," Trey pulled Candi close to him.

Candi kissed Trey before getting interrupted by the knock at the door.

"I'll get that, that's probably my Grand Mariner and chocolate cover strawberries."

Candi opened the door, and Katie let herself in as she ignored Candi.

"Trey, you made me look like a fool in court today," Katie said as she started toward him.

"Katie, why are you here and how did you get past my men?" Trey asked, standing in front of her shirtless and confused.

"I used my charm. You forget I'm a cop's daughter," she replied, flashing the Taser she used on both men.

"Honey, you need to leave. I don't think your Fed buddies would approve of this visit," Candi said.

"Not until Trey hears me out," Katie replied in an agitated state.

"I'm calling security," Candi replied as she picked up the phone to dial the front desk. "Bitch, put the fuckin' phone down!" Katie yelled as she pulled a gun out of her purse. "Calm down, Katie. Look, let Candi leave the room. I'm the one you came for."

"I don't give a fuck about this man stealing hoe."

"Say what! Who are you calling a hoe?"

Trey grabbed Candi to keep her from charging Katie.

Katie cocked her gun.

"Come get you some, missy. You know your wife really deserves better. I should kill this bitch and you."

"Katie, why are you doing this?"

"Why you ask? It wasn't enough that you used me like a whore. You dated me just to rub it in my father's face. You killed my brother, my mother and my father. I knew you were an animal, but I thought you had some sort of dignity. You never loved me. You embarrassed me in front of the world like I was some spiteful bitch."

"Look Katie, please stop waving that gun. I did care for you."

"Lair!" She yelled as she fired the gun, hitting Trey in the shoulder.

"Oh my God!" Candi screamed.

Katie fired two more shots hitting Trey in the chest.

"This is one sentence you can't buy your way out of."

Candi charged Katie fearing she was planning to shoot her as well. As the two of them struggled for control of the gun, Katie got the upper hand.

"Please don't kill me," Candi begged while stumbling to the floor.

"As much as I want to shoot you for stealing Trey from me four years ago, I want you to live to tell why I did it," Katie said as she turned the gun on herself.

"Katie, no!" Candi yelled as Katie shot herself in the chest.

The gunfire finally awakened Trey body guards. They broke down the door and saw Trey laying on the floor bleeding. They knew they had made a huge mistake letting Katie get the drop on them. Hotel security finally arrived.

"Please call 911! We need an ambulance!" Candi yelled.

She kneeled next to Katie feeling sorry for her. Katie held Candi's hand. "You tell them I had nothing left when he killed my parents. His lawyer took the little self-respect I had from me today. Now, I can be with my family," Katie said spitting up blood.

"Katie, I'm so sorry."

"I forgive you. I only hope Monica will do the same. I've had pain in my heart for so long. Now I can finally rest in peace. Isn't it fitting that out of everyone who has tried, I'm the one to dethrone the King of the Streets." Katie closed her eyes as her heart stopped beating.

Candi was in shock after witnessing Katie die. It hit her that Trey was gone. She covered her eyes in disbelief. Crawling to his side, she kissed him on the cheek as he lay motionless. Paramedics arrived and found Candi hovering over Trey, crying profusely. After determining that Katie was DOA, the paramedics turned their focus to Trey.

"Miss, let us see if we can save him."

"You are too late. You're too late!" She screamed.

The two medics attended to Trey. "I got a weak pulse," one of the medics said as they rushed to get him strapped down and ready to transport.

The police arrived on the scene as the medics rushed Trey out to the ambulance.

*   *   *   *   *

At County Memorial, Trey was in critical condition. Candi was giving her statement to the police outside the waiting room when she saw Monica and Ms. Wilkens enter the waiting area.

This is going to be really awkward, Candi thought to herself.

"Please, I need to know, is my son okay?" Ms. Wilkens asked in an obvious emotional state.

"Miss, what's your son's name?" the receptionist asked.

"Trey Wilkens."

"Ms. Wilkens, all I can tell you at the moment is he is in surgery. Dr. Ponte is one of the finest trauma surgeons in Chicago. As soon as we have any updates, I will let you know immediately."

"Thank you," Monica replied as they found a place to sit.

Monica spotted Candi finishing up her conversation with the policemen.

"Ms. Wilkens, excuse me for a moment. Let me find out what she knows about this ordeal."

Monica approached Candi, figuring she could provide some answers to what happened. "Hi Candi, I heard you were back in town. I should have known the moment I told Trey I was filing for a divorce you would race to his side."

"Monica I..."

"Honey, you can save the explanation because I really don't give a shit. All I want to know is what happened?"

"Katie came to Trey's hotel room and forced her way in and shot him three times before turning the gun on herself."

"Wow, and she let you live to tell it all. Damn the luck," Monica said sarcastically before turning to walk away.

*   *   *   *   *

Hours later, Dr. Ponte entered the waiting room.

"Wilkens family?"

Monica, Ms. Wilkens and Candi all stepped forward.

"Honey, you're not a Wilkens," Elaine said to Candi.

"It's okay, let her stay. If it wasn't for her he probably wouldn't be alive," Monica added.

"Okay, well I'm Dr. Ponte. Trey is doing rather well considering being shot several times. I successfully removed the bullets, and he is in stable condition. He did lose a lot of blood and is very weak. Amazingly, no major damage was sustained."

"Thank the Lord!" Ms. Wilkens shouted.

"When can we see him?" Monica asked.

"He's in recovery at this point. We will hold him there for observation for a couple hours before transferring him to ICU. Typically, we do not let family members enter the recovery unit, but I will make an exception. I can only allow one family member at a time go in to see him."

* * * * *

Monica entered the recovery room after letting Ms. Wilkens spend her time with him. She approached his beside and touches his hand.

"Trey, things have really gone from bad to worse fast. Why couldn't we have had a normal life together? You know I love you with all my heart. It's just this right here right now is what I can't handle. Please, if not for me, give up this lifestyle to be here to watch your son grow up." Trey clutched Monica's fingers as he attempted to open his eyes. Monica kissed his cheek.

"Don't try and talk, save your strength. I'm sure someone else will be happy to know you have awakened. I will send her in."

CHAPTER 17

RETURN OF THE KING

At an undisclosed location Half-Dead continued to beat on Shante.

"If you plan to kill me then do it and get it over with," Shante said spitting out blood.

"As tempting as that sounds, that would be too good for you. Besides, not until Trey gives the orders."

"Look man, I thought Trey and I had a deal. He stepped down and put me in charge of things. So why am I being held against my will by you two fools?"

Half-Dead punched Shante again in his badly bruised face. "Maybe if we keep punching you, your memory will come back."

"Damn dog, you had to have it all. Did you really think you could be the man? Your cousin Deek fucked up. Not only did he get his ass kicked, right about now Deek should be getting introduced to the meaning of gang raped. Don't worry though, after he's been violated over and over again, he'll be begging for someone to take him out his misery."

*   *   *   *   *

In Judge Waters' chambers, both counselors were meeting to discuss the proceedings of the case.

"Your Honor, obviously from the unforeseen events that took place, my client was a victim of circumstances. He is unable to stand trial today."

"Would you like a continuance?"

"Actually Your Honor, I would like to request a dismissal of all
charges against my client. My client was entrapped by Katie Turner
who was working with the federal authorities. He was held against his
will at gunpoint and forced to confess to a crime he did not commit
just to save his life. This woman was obviously disturbed, and based
on her actions, the state's key witness' testimony should be removed
from the case. She attempted to kill my client and later took her own
life in the process."

"This doesn't change the fact that two officers and six men were
killed," Nina responded.

"I'm glad you brought that up. The state's only evidence was tainted.
Here is the copy of the ballistics' report I just received this morning.
Forensic findings show that the bullets removed from Sgt. Turner
matches Lt. Dawson's gun. The bullets removed from Lt. Dawson
matches Sgt. Turner's gun. Forensic Specialist Christopher Swells is
here today to testify on the findings. As far as the other men, you have
no physical evidence that my client was involved in the shooting or for
that matter was even at the scene of the crime. The two officers
involved died at the scene. It would appear that one officer turned on
the other while making a drug bust. The briefcase filled with 10 kilos
of cocaine lying next to them supports this theory."

"Are you seriously accusing one of the officers of being a dirty cop?"

"Here's what I think happened. During the officer's drug bust, Lt.
Dawson turned on Sgt. Turner, and they both shot each other. The
ballistic reports definitely indicate that there was foul play at the scene.
By the way, I also have sworn affidavits from two real estate investors

which confirm that during the time of the shooting, my client was in a meeting regarding a potential business venture halfway across town."

"You and I both know those affidavits are bogus. The recording clearly supports him being at the scene and killing Lt. Dawson."

"Again, if that is your argument then you clearly have no case. The recording was declared inadmissible evidence. Counselor, if someone held you at gunpoint and threatened to kill you unless you admitted to a crime, you'd probably do the same."

"I would never confess to a crime knowing I'm innocent. With that being said, I'm not on trial your client is," Nina paused while she continued to review the documents. "Counselor, you're not going to force me to rule on this, are you?"

"No Your Honor, at this time to save the state further embarrassment, I move to dismiss all the charges against the defendant."

"Very well, I will dismiss."

Nina knew Trey was involved, but the ballistic reports and sworn affidavits along with Katie's attempt on Trey's life was too damaging to her case. Unfortunately, she had nothing to proceed with.

*   *   *   *   *

Ashcroft entered Trey's hospital room as he was signing his release papers.

"Not even a few bullets can stop you," Ashcroft said jokingly.

Trey was sitting up on the bed shirtless, with his right shoulder and chest heavily bandaged.

"So, I take it you were able to get a continuance?"

"Not exactly, the copy of the ballistics reports from the shooting and

Katie's actions pretty much backed the D.A. into a corner. Trey
Wilkens my man, you are a free man. The state of Illinois has dropped
all charges against you."

"Damn, are you serious?"

"No joke, my friend," Ashcroft answered shaking Trey's hand.

"It seems that prayer Pastor Thomas did on my behalf definitely paid
off."

"Apparently, before I forget, you need to thank Bradford & Anderson,
LLC for the affidavits they provided."

"I will definitely send them a care package."

"I knew you left the drugs at the scene to pin the shooting on Lt.
Dawson. When I got the ballistics report and read the results, I was
stunned."

"I picked up Sgt. Turner's gun while they were fighting over Lt.
Dawson's weapon. I figured since Richard was dead set on killing the
man responsible for his wife's death, I owed him that much
considering all him and I been through. Besides, after seeing him
double-cross his partner, I knew sooner or later he would do the same
to me. He wanted to be me so I showed him what this life is truly
about. Drugs, money and double-crosses."

"Well, you've definitely made me earn my keep. Now do me a favor
and stay out of trouble. Hopefully, the next time my office hear from
you, it'll be to finalize your business contracts," Ashcroft said as he
exited the room.

* * * * *

Monica walked out of the bathroom with her bath towel wrapped around her. She was startled by Trey's presence.

"Trey, what are you doing here?"

"I still live here. I figured my first act as a free man should be to see my wife and son."

"I wasn't aware that you were being released from the hospital so soon."

"Well, I don't like hospitals, and between the pain killers and the bandages, I will be fine. But that's not what I meant. The state dropped all charges against me."

"Well I guess congratulations are in order."

"Pastor Thomas stopped by the hospital this morning and shared your concerns for me."

Monica put on her robe, dropping the damp bath towel. "It's nothing that I haven't already shared with you. Trey, why are you really here?"

"Truthfully, I was hoping with this trial behind me, maybe we could reconcile our marriage."

Monica sat on the bed and applied lotion to her legs.

"It is clear to me that you have very little respect for me and Candi. Even after you posted bail before getting shot, you stayed at the club sleeping with Candi. Not one time did you call or come home to see me or your son. It's been hell here. All the camera crews and paparazzi swarming my every move, day after day has been too much to handle. I meant what I said. I can't do this anymore."

Trey approached Monica and opened her robe and stared at her nude body. He pushed her back on the bed and attempted to climb on top of her.

"What are you doing?"

Trey kissed Monica's neck and despite her unwillingness to be with him, he touched her spot, and she momentarily got caught up in her sexual needs.

"Trey, no."

Trey rubbed her sweet spot as he slowly slid down toward it. Before she knew it, she could feel his tongue between her legs. Monica arched her back and closed her eyes as Trey licked her cherry. She clutched the bed sheets.

"Trey, please stop."

Trey stopped momentarily, but only to pull off his pants. Monica still lying on the bed with her eyes closed, breathed a sigh of relief that he respected her wishes and pulled back. As she opened her eyes, Trey climbed on top of her.

"Trey, wait a minute, we are not doing this."

Monica tried to push him off but he continued to force himself on her. He pushed himself inside of her and grabbed her hands. Monica laid still and allowed Trey to fuck her. She began to cry. Trey was feeling good about himself and began grunting as he ejaculated inside Monica. He suddenly realized Monica's tears were not from pleasure.

"Baby, what's wrong?" He asked after kissing her.

"Get off of me."

Trey allowed Monica to get up.

"Monica, I want us to pick up where we left off. I told you I will keep my promise and be the husband you deserve."

Monica felt cheap and dirty. She closed her robe as she watched Trey put on his pants. "You had to have me, even after I told you no. Well I hope you enjoyed it because that was the last time you will ever get a piece of this cookie. How do you think Candi would feel if she knew you forced yourself on me?"

"I don't give a damn about what Candi thinks. She is my past, and you are my wife. It is your job to please me. If I recall, you seem to be enjoying yourself when I was licking you. Now you have turned this shit into some rape bullshit."

"Trey, I told you I didn't want this but just forget it. I just hope Candi don't have any diseases. This changes nothing between us. I'm still filing for a divorce."

"Why are you being so stubborn? Is this your way of punishing me?"

"Trey, you are not listening to me. I don't want you and this marriage anymore. Please, just leave and don't come back," Monica demanded as tears ran down her face. Trey approached her, attempting to console her. "Please don't touch me. Don't you think you've done enough?"

"Okay fine, I'll leave. If this is what you truly want."

"Yes, it is."

Trey removed his door key from his key chain and dropped it on the bed.

"If you need me, you know where I will be."

"I do, with Candi."

"Have your lawyer contact mine. Hopefully we can work out visitation," Trey added before leaving.

* * * * *

Trey was sitting at his desk when Calvin and Big Earl, the club bouncers, escorted three men into Trey's office.

"So, I understand you guys want to work for me."

"Yes sir. It would be an honor," Turk answered.

"Well then, have a seat," Trey added.

"Trey, I'm Kelvin, Candi's brother."

"I know who you are. It came to my attention that you guys carried out a hit on Sgt. Turner to impress me." Kelvin smiled feeling proud about what they did.

"We figured if we could eliminate the thorn in your side, you would put us on. Besides, that cop that paid us said you were on board with it."

Calvin forcefully put his hand on Kelvin's shoulder shoving him back in the chair. "Really, that's what he said? Well the next time you three decide to help me, you should make sure you finish what you start. Because of you three monkeys, I have a couple of bullet holes in my chest. You killed the man's wife and sent him on a rampage. He blamed me for her death and came gunning for me. So, forgive me if I'm not appreciative of the help you three provided. Kelvin, because you are Candi's brother I'm gonna give you three a pass, just this one time."

"Thank you, Trey," Kelvin responded.

"Don't thank me yet, because my first thought was to have your bodies dumped in the Mississippi River. If I get any more heat from this shit you three better be on the first thing smoking to Alaska. Earl, get these bitches out of my office."

* * * * *

Trey entered his hotel suite. Candi was stretched out across the king size bed watching TV.

"I hope you didn't mind me letting myself in?"

"No problem."

"It's all over the news about the D.A. dropping the charges against you."

Trey poured himself a drink at the bar. He took a sip before responding. "I went by the house to see Monica."

"How did it go?"

"Well, she made it clear that she doesn't want anything else to do with me."

Candi turned off the TV and joined Trey at the bar. She poured herself a drink.

"How does that make you feel?"

"Candi, I love my wife. Kind of ironic, I never thought I would be sitting here telling you that I am heartbroken."

"Trey, I understand. I know you love her. She's the mother of your child."

"Monica is a lot more than that. I guess I can't blame her considering all the shit I put her through."

"Trey, I know you need time to work through this. I can leave if you need to be alone."

"No, don't leave. I want you to stay."

* * * * *

Shante stared at Trey as he entered the room. Crazy Willie and Half-Dead were the supporting cast as Trey stood in front of Shante.

"Finally, you rose up from the hospital bed and decided to grace me with your presence."

"Funny, even strapped to the chair smelling like sweat and piss, you still got a sense of humor. I guess these guys didn't beat it out of you."

"Well, let's get this over with. If you're going to kill me then go ahead. I'm not afraid to die."

"Relax, I see you are a get straight down to business kind of guy. I respect that but can a brother take some time to give you your just due? Your scheme to have me killed in Greenville was pretty clever. Just like Meechi, you proved you can't be trusted."

"Fuck you! You're speaking on trust. You killed my brother. How do you expect me to get past that?"

"I thought we had moved past that situation. Apparently, it was foolish of me to think we could. I took some time off and handed you the keys to my kingdom. In the back of my mind, I knew one day you would make a play. In this game, you have to expect the unexpected. Well the king has returned. You had your shot, now it's my turn."

Trey pulled his gun out and shot Shante in both knees. Shante screamed out in pain.

"Untie his bitch ass and bring him to the back."

Half-Dead and Crazy Willie untied Shante and dragged him into the warehouse. "Shante, I got something really special planned for you."

Trey walked toward the cage and unlocked it. Shante saw the two huge white Siberian tigers. Trey petted one of the tigers as he gestured for the men to bring Shante to the cage.

"I would like for you to meet Mandy and Milo. I feel kind of bad because I haven't fed them in two days. They both should be really hungry. You know, Milo really likes his meat bloody," Trey said as he shot Shante in the chest.

"Trey wait, don't do this please! I promise to never cross you again."

"I know."

Trey watched as Shante got shoved into the cage and the tigers wasted little time ripping into him.

"Damn, that was brutal," Crazy Willie commented.

"Fellows, I have one more job for the two of you," Trey handed both guys an envelope with twenty thousand dollars enclosed.

"As usual, you've peaked my curiosity," Half-Dead replied as he thumbed through the hundreds.

"I need you guys to pay a visit to this Special Agent that got off on the wrong foot with me during my visit to Greenville."

"We will take care of it," Crazy Willie answered.

Trey handed Crazy Willie a folder. Crazy Willie opened it and looked at the photo of the man.

"His address is on the back of the photo. Don't kill him, just send him a message. He needs to realize that I always deliver on a promise."

www.ingramcontent.com/pod-product-compliance
Lightning Source LLC
Chambersburg PA
CBHW061207170626
46809CB00003B/1276